Mommy Saves the Day

An MDLG themed story of Mommy Dom Carol, who was looking for a cheeky ABDL girl...little did she know her world was about to be turned upside down by little Ivy

By Tina Moore

Table of Contents

Chapter 1

Ivy didn't care about other people. She didn't have the luxury of feeling the emotions that went with being one of those 'helpful' people. After growing up in the system, she had changed her name the moment she turned 18. She considered it her birthday gift to herself, a kind of rebirth if you like. She had done other things as well. Like cut and dye her hair, from long and blonde to should length and jet black, the way her heartfelt. She left the house where she had only just been placed in and jumped on the first bus out of town. She didn't really know what she was going to do, all she knew was that no one cared about her, so she didn't have to care about anyone but herself.

"Wake up, kid, you have to get off now," a man said, gently shaking Ivy awake. She grabbed her ripped backpack and walked off the bus, stopping and sitting down on the seats at the terminal and watched the bus drive off.

Well, you're here now. The place you said you'd always get to. I mean, this was always the plan, even if you have no idea what you are going to do next, she thought to herself as she sat there. She hadn't thought of a plan besides, get out of town, and as she checked her phone, she wasn't surprised that nobody had called her for her birthday.

Why would you even bother checking? You know that they don't give a shit about you. They never have, you were always just a paycheck to them. But you don't have to think about that anymore. You know what the plan is. You know how you're going to get everything that you have ever dreamed about. So it's time to put all that shit to the side and decide that you are going to have a good life regardless of the shitty start you've had, she thought to herself as she got up and walked out of the bus terminal and into her new life.

Carol cracked her neck and thanked a higher source that is was Friday. She was a nurse at a plastic surgeon practice and loved the regular working hours. After years of shift work, the most alluring aspect of the job was that she could maintain a 'standard' work-life balance. Carol was older than the young nurses she worked with and enjoyed their youthful and playful personalities. They had taken to calling her Mama, something that she both enjoyed and found somewhat frustrating. The problem Carol had with it was that she was a Mommy Dom, not that any of those girls would be able to tell. She didn't overly dominate them, even when she had to correct their behavior, she never told them what to do in a demeaning way, but she did care for them. She would make cakes for birthdays and organize staff dinners and events. She shared with them recipes and had even helped one of the girls move house when she got kicked out by her boyfriend.

"Hey, Mama, can you help me word this

ad. It needs to be put in the job-seeking section of the website, and I don't really know what to say," one of the girls asked Carol as they were eating lunch.

"Sure. How about this afternoon when it's a little quieter?" Carol replied, enjoying how the girl's tight work uniform hugged her slim figure.

"Thanks, Mama, sounds perfect," the girl excitedly said as she got up, placing a hand on Carol's shoulder as she walked back into the building. Carol could feel herself slipping into her Mommy space, and she tightened her calves and loudly exhaled as she fought herself back out of that space.

Not right now, you can go home and think about her all you want, but that's not what she is after, and you can't manipulate her into a situation that you want, but she doesn't, but you can sure think about her, Carol said to herself as she finished her lunch.

And that is exactly what she did. Carol lay down

on her bed after a warm shower and ran her hands over her body, imagining that it was her young co-worker, timidly touching her for the first time.

"Like this?" She imagined the slender brunette almost whispering as Carol guided her closer to her pussy.

"Yes, baby. Be a good girl and stick out your tongue for Mommy," Carol imagined herself replying as she thought of how she would hold the girl's face in her hands and rub her wet pussy over the girl's mouth, feeling her hot tongue against her clit.

"Fuck me," Carol angrily moaned out loud as she opened her eyes and groaned in frustration. She got up and began putting on her lingerie, annoyed that her daydream was better than her reality. She decided that she needed to go for a walk, so putting on her activewear, Carol headed out into the Friday afternoon sun.

Ivy had spent the first three nights in the big new

city in a motel. She had worked two jobs since she had turned 15 and had managed to save enough money to last her a few months, but she knew that she needed to find a job and fast. Having spent the day handing out resumes to diners and gas stations, Ivy had ended up in a coffee shop, drinking a white chocolate latte and taking small bites of a choc chip cookie.

This is what life could be like. Going to work, even though I don't have a job yet, and then coming to cool cafes and enjoying all these things you've only ever seen in magazines, she thought to herself as she watched the people walk by and wondered what kind of lives they led. She had always enjoyed doing this. She had thought it was because she was learning how to behave in the world; it wasn't like her foster families were ever interested in helping her make sense of the world. Ivy reached down for her backpack at the same time as Carol walked past her, causing Carol's knee to run straight into Ivy's head.

"Oh darling, I am so sorry, are you alright?!" Carol said as Ivy gasped in pain, placing her hand over her head and biting her bo. Ivy frowned and ground her teeth. She knew that she shouldn't tell this woman to go to hell though that was what her first thought was.

"Yeah, I'm fine," Ivy said, looking at Carol dead in the eye and almost having to catch her breath. Never in her 18 years had she been near somebody with the warm, loving energy that she felt from the woman in front of her, and it pierced the numbing condition Ivy had cloaked around herself.

"Are you sure?" Carol questioned, slightly frowning as Ivy tried to get up, only to become dizzy and fall back into her seat. It felt all too much for Ivy, who noticed the world begin to spin as she looked up at Carol, who reached out to touch the large bump which was forming on Ivy's forehead.

"Should we call an ambulance?" A waitress asked. That was the last thing Ivy heard before her whole world turned black.

Chapter 2

"Hey there," Carol said to Ivy, who looked around, frightened at the unfamiliar surroundings.

"It's ok, honey, you're in the hospital. You passed out in the café. We looked into your purse. Ivy, is it?" Carol said as Ivy sat up, wincing.

"Yeah," Ivy replied, frowning as she saw the strange woman again. A nurse walked into the room and handed Ivy her discharge papers, placing them on the bedside before giving Ivy a fake smile and walking out. Ivy hated women like that nurse who always seemed to look down on her because she can from trash.

"I wish you hadn't of called an ambulance. I kinda can't afford any of this," Ivy said timidly, embarrassed and beginning to blush. She felt a knot in her stomach begin to form as she thought about how she was going to get out of this situation. She knew that she wasn't in a position to run, her head still hurt way too much, but she also knew that even with all her savings, she wouldn't be able to pay for these medical bills. Ivy just looked up at Carol, who was smiling at Ivy in a way that Ivy couldn't understand. She hadn't seen the expression that was on Carol's face directed toward her before, and it made her uncomfortable because she didn't know how to respond.

"Sweetheart, I am the one who put you in here. So, of course, I've already taken care of the bill. I can't begin to tell you how sorry I am. Your family must be worried sick about you, is there someone I can call for you?" Carol said, making Ivy suspicious and wary. In her 18 years of experience, when people did kind things for her, they always wanted something in return, but as if reading her mind, Carol smiled.

"You don't owe me a thing, Ivy. It was just the right thing to do. I had no idea how hard my knees where," Carol said, causing Ivy to giggle despite herself.

Ivy filled in the paperwork and made her way to the front of the hospital.

"Can I offer you a ride home?" Carol asked, seeing Ivy looking confused as she tried to orientate herself.

"Um, no, it's cool I can manage. You've been more than amazing. Thanks for everything," Ivy said, hailing a taxi that just drove past her. It was late, far later than Ivy liked being out, and the cold night air made her shiver.

"Come on, there'll be no cabs here for a while yet," Carol said, smiling warmly. Ivy hated herself for feeling so drawn to this woman, but she rolled her eyes and followed Carol toward her car.

"Seatbelts," Carol said once Ivy was sitting in her luxury SUV. It was the type of car that Ivy had only seen in magazines.

No wonder she could afford my medical bills, this bitch is rich as fuck, Ivy thought to herself as she put on her seatbelt.

"So, where is home, honey?" Carol asked, turning the heating up as she saw Ivy thin arms covered in goosebumps.

"Um. So I'm staying in a motel at the moment. It's the Lucky Star. Do you know it? I can find it on my phone," Ivy said, biting her bottom lip and quickly finding it for Carol.

"You're a little young to be on your own, aren't you?" Carol asked as she drove toward the motel.

"I'm the oldest I've ever been," Ivy smugly replied, causing Carol to laugh. Ivy found it strange that Carol didn't seem phased by her hostile, sarcastic remarks and smiled to herself, enjoying that Carol wasn't offended by her snarkiness. Ivy had a tendency to push people away when they got too close, and she liked that Carol didn't seem phased by her attempts to push her away. If Ivy was being honest, she didn't really want Carol to go. She just wasn't sure if she could trust her.

"Well, I can't dispute that. But not many 18-year-olds stay in a motel on the outskirts of town, do they?" Carol replied, causing Ivy to lift her knees to her chest.

"Guess not," Ivy replied, putting her knees back down when Carol gently patted them.

"Sorry," Ivy said, turning to look out the window. Carol looked at the rough diamond sitting in her passenger seat. Ivy's black hair was tied up in a half bun, her skinny black jeans had rips in the knees, and her baggy t-shirt with the sleeves folded up made her heart swell. Her chipped crimson nail polish and worn out black leather combat boots added to her look, and Carol wondered how long it would be before Ivy was on the streets.

She is just a picture of cuteness that's for sure. A little bit on the young side, I couldn't even take her to a bar. But look at those sad little eyes, Carol thought, wishing she could find a way to keep Ivy.

"Do you want to get something to eat, or

whatever?" Ivy asked suddenly, turning to face Carol. The look on the older woman's face made Ivy feel safe, an unusual feeling for her, and made her beg to a higher being that Carol didn't say no.

"That would be nice. Where are you thinking? What do you like?" Carol asked, laughing at the face Ivy pulled.

"What do I like? Um, food?" Ivy replied as Carol pulled into a diner a few minutes from the motel. Ivy had never been one to be a picky eater, mostly because she never really knew when her next meal was coming and secondly because even if she knew, the options were slim.

"So here would be fine?" Carol asked as Ivy raised her eyebrows and nodded. Carol pulled into the diner parking lot and looked around. It wasn't the sort of place she would choose if it was her choice, and she tried to look relaxed about leaving her SUV out in the open, deciding that she needed to make sure they got a window seat so that she could make sure that her

SUV wasn't stolen.

"Ok," Carol said more to herself than to Ivy as she got out of the car and walked inside.

"Just, try not to give me concussion this time, yeah?" Ivy teased as they sat down.

"I will do my best," Carol replied, making Ivy laugh. Carol didn't want to feel herself entering Mommy space but as she sat in the booth opposite Ivy in all her youthful glory, it was hard not to.

"I'll take the pancakes, a chocolate shake, the cheeseburger and fries, and a soda. Thanks," Ivy said, ignoring the expression on Carol's face.

"What?" Ivy asked when Carol ordered the fish and salad.

"Nothing, it's not my place to judge," Carol replied, only causing Ivy to become more annoyed.

"Hey, what's your name anyway?" Ivy asked, realizing that she didn't know the name of the woman sitting in front of her.

"Oh, sorry. I'm Carol," she replied,

extending her hand playfully. Ivy took it and felt something like electricity pulse through her veins, holding onto Carol's hand for longer than necessary.

"And to answer your question from before. I left the home I was last put in. That's why I am out here alone," Ivy said, watching the cars drive passed the diner.

"Were you in foster care?" Carol gently asked, not wanting to upset Ivy, who just nodded her head.

"And this. This is because I sort of only eat once a day," Ivy added after her order was placed in front of her.

"Why once a day?" Carol asked as Ivy began to devour her pancakes.

"Because. I have a food budget of about $12 a day for food, and there's no fridge in the motel," Ivy explained, surprised that Carol could get so much information out of her so easily.

"Are you working?" Carol asked as she ate her fish. Ivy just shook her head.

"My whole plan was to move here, find a job and save up for a place to rent," Ivy said, looking at Carol, who just smiled back at her.

"I think it's very brave and stoic what you are doing, sweetheart," Carol said, making Ivy just smile and scoff at her compliment.

"Yeah, well. I didn't want to end up being just another fucking loser, did I?" Ivy said, enjoying the shock on Carol's face.

"Language, young lady!" Carol playful said, making Ivy smile like a naughty girl getting into trouble. She had to admit. There was something about Carol, which she liked even if she didn't know how to describe the feeling.

"Would you take my number? So that if you need somebody for, I don't know, anything you have someone in this crazy city to call? I'm sure you don't need anyone, you're clearly able to look after yourself, but it might be nice to have a friend here," Carol said, offering Ivy her business card. Ivy looked at Carol for a moment, unsure whether to take the card or not.

"You don't have to ring if you don't want to. But I would feel better knowing that you aren't alone here. Would you take it for me?" Carol said, Ivy tentatively reaching out to take her card.

"The motel is only a block away from here. I can walk it. Thanks for everything," Ivy said as Carol walked to her car.

"Honey, the only people who are out this late, are hookers, and girls that pimps want to turn into hookers. I'm not letting them get their hands on you. Get in the car," Carol said, making Ivy laugh at how her voice made her sound more dominant.

"Fine," Ivy said. She bit her lip as Carol leaned into the car and buckled her into the seat. Ivy knew that her eyes were giving her away, but she couldn't help it. As much as she tried to hide it, Carol turned her on. She wasn't sure if it was her whole, I'll protect you from the world thing, or the fact that Ivy hadn't felt seen in her whole life, but whatever it was, it was working. Carol noticed Ivy involuntarily spread her thighs, and her breathing became shallow as Carol closed in the distance between then. She felt her own clit begin to tingle with desire and fought herself not to reach behind Ivy's head and kiss her passionately. Carol stepped back and licked her lips before pulling her hair to one side and walked to the driver's side.

"Plus, I like having you around, you're fun with your moody little attitude," Carol laughed as she drove out of the parking lot.

Carol had dropped Ivy home as she had promised, but when Ivy lingered at the door, Carol offered if she wanted her to come inside. Carol had all but swooned when Ivy timidly nodded her head. Ivy knew she was a lesbian, but she had never allowed herself to try anything, but there was something about Carol that made her feel as though she wasn't in control of herself anymore.

"I um, guess I should have kept it a little

tidier," Ivy said, blushing as she collected her things and placed them in the corner on a chair. Looking around the room, uncertainty in her eyes, Carol sat down on the edge of the bed and patted for Ivy to join her.

"I've never done this. Like any of this," Ivy nervously said, Carol, reaching out and running her fingers through Ivy's hair.

"Yeah, I sort of figured," Carol loving replied. They sat in silence, Carol wondering if this was a good idea after all. Ivy hesitantly reached out and put her hand on Carol's thigh.

"Can I kiss you?" Ivy asked so quietly that Carol almost didn't hear it. Smiling warmly, Carol nodded and took the lead. Placing a hand on either side of Ivy's face and bringing her lips down on the younger girl's lips, gently at first, then more passionately as she felt Ivy gain confidence. Ivy moaned as she pushed against Carol's mouth, her body turning hot before she pulled away, panting.

"It's ok. We don't have to do anymore,

honey," Carol said, reading the look in Ivy's eyes. The fire, the fear, the desire, and the caution. Ivy just stood up in front of Carol, her thighs straddling Carol's as she slowly took her t-shirt off, revealing her thin frame, her slightly protruding ribs and perky b-cup breasts in a black lace bra.

"You are so beautiful, baby," Carol breathlessly said, getting caught off guard by how angelic Ivy looked. Running her hands over Ivy's body, Ivy wrapped her arms around Carol's neck and melted into her. Feeling Carol's heavy, soft breasts against her tummy, Ivy grinded on her lap, making soft sounds as she continued to give in to desire.

"I want to feel you," Ivy softly said as she began to pull on Carol's clothes, making her laugh.

"Just wait a moment, sugar. Let's get under the covers. You're getting cold," Carol said, using Ivy's cool skin as an excuse to hide her body. Although she was not ashamed of her figure, she didn't want to turn Ivy off by her body. Ivy stood up, peeled back the covers and giggled as Carol pushed her into bed and onto her back.

"Hey," Ivy said, in a little voice, half surprising herself. She hadn't remembered a time she had felt this happy or free and safe as Carol scooped her up in her arms and kissed her.

"Hey, honey," Carol lovingly said in her Mommy voice. Ivy snuggled into her as she stroked her back and grabbed the waistband on her jeans, pulling her up, higher on her ass.

"I think these need to come off," Carol whispered, making Ivy laugh.

"What about this?" Ivy replied, pulling on Carol's shirt.

"Well, it's only fair," Carol replied, letting Ivy take it off. Carol watched Ivy's eyes as she took everything in, enjoying how her timid touch made goosebumps over her body. Ivy stroked the top of Carol's breasts, enjoying how soft and warm her skin was before wriggling up to kiss her once again. Ivy felt Carol wrap her arms around her and rolled Ivy over to have her laying on top of her.

"I um," Ivy said as she pinned Carol down by her shoulders.

"It's ok, sweetie, we don't have too," Carol replied, reading Ivy's eyes and allowing herself to be dominated, knowing that Ivy needed to feel empowered and in control.

"It's not you, it's just, um," Ivy started to explain as Carol began to shake her head, stopping Ivy from continuing.

"It's just that you wanted to, and now you don't. And it's that simple honey, and anyone who can't handle that needs to take a good hard look at why they have such high rape traits," Carol replied, watching as Ivy sucked her own thumb and lay down on top of Carol.

"You don't need to apologize, beautiful," Carol continued as she felt Ivy snuggle into her cleavage. Ivy thought back to all the times she had told someone no, and they hadn't listened. It made her heart hurt and tears well up in her eyes.

Why didn't they care as much as Carol does, Ivy thought to herself as she felt Carol begin to stroke her back and gently pat her bottom as she fell asleep.

Chapter 3

"Morning girls," Carol beamed Monday morning. Gabi and Hope, some of the girls' Carol worked with looked up, suspicion written all over their faces.

"You're overly happy today, Mama. Do we even want to know what you got up to on the weekend?!" Hope giggled as Carol put her things away.

"No. And even if you did want to know, I don't kiss and tell," Carol teased as she got on with her day, leaving the girls full of curiosity.

"Hey, I hope it is ok that I called," Ivy softly said down the phone. Carol had told her that her lunch break was usually around one in the afternoon, and as Carol had her lunch, she felt herself enter her Mommy space as she listened to Ivy's sweet voice.

"Not at all, darling," Carol replied, instantly feeling her pussy tighten with desire.

"Ok, great," Ivy said, unsure of what else to say, but wanting to hear Carol's voice.

"How are you?" Carol said, filling the space that began to fill between them. Ivy had heard back from the diner where she and Carol had first spent time together.

"Good. I got a job, at that diner we went to," Ivy replied, pride in her voice that her plan was coming to fruition.

"Well done, baby!" Carol exclaimed, delighted for Ivy.

"I hope you aren't working the late shifts though," Carol quickly added, thinking of all the unsavory remarks Ivy was no doubt about to hear.

"Well, I have a few of them. But that's fine, I need the money, and they give you a free drink with every shift," Ivy replied happily. Carol looked around to see that Gabi and Hope were both watching her with amusement in their eyes, and Carol rolled her eyes at them, making them giggle.

"We should do something to celebrate. Are you free tonight?" Carol asked. Ivy had never had anyone celebrate her achievements before, and it made her feel wonderful.

"Um, yeah I am actually, I start next week. So, I'm all yours," Ivy replied, a hint of seduction in her voice, making Carol swoon.

"Great. I'll pick you up at seven, and I'll keep where we are going a surprise, but I think you'll like it," Carol said, giving Ivy knots of excitement and anticipation in her stomach. Hanging up the phone, Ivy looked at the clothing options she still had available and frowned.

I really need to do some washing, she thought, opening her purse to find a few dollars' worth of coins. Checking the time, she rushed out the door, knowing that she wanted to make sure her body was perfectly shaven and her make up flawless for her date tonight.

"Who was that?" Gabi asked as Carol

passed them.

"My date," Carol said rather impressed that Ivy seemed to enjoy her company as much as she did hers.

"How young is this one?" Hope teased. It was common knowledge that Carol liked younger women, and the girls she worked with had often joked about it with her. Carol didn't mind; in fact, it turned her on. She had gone hoe countless times and fucked herself thinking of how she would put them over her knee and spank them until they weren't giggling anymore, or filling their mouths with her nipple and dressing them in sweet little onesies.

"She's a baby, that's for sure," Carol replied, amused that her response had multiple meanings.

"Knock knock," Carol said as she leaned against the opened door to Ivy's motel room.

"Hey," Ivy happily said, turning around and making Carol's heart swell as she looked into

Ivy's big green eyes.

"Hi, sweetie," Carol said, walking into the room and taking the girl in her arms.

"Mm, you smell divine," Carol said, nuzzling into Ivy's neck and making her giggle.

"It's just body spray," Ivy replied, pushing Carol away and grabbing her purse. Carol held out her hand dramatically, making Ivy look at her with those big innocent eyes as she took Carol's hand, and they walked to the car.

"So, where are we going?" Ivy asked, her tight black dress hugging her body was draped in a black denim jacket, and Carol noticed that she was once again wearing her combat boots. Her hair was shaken out, and the layers made her look particularly street cool.

"Well, I noticed how much you liked burgers. So I am taking you to an all you can eat burger place where you can design your own burgers. It will probably make me put on five kilos, but it'll be worth it to see what type of creations you come up with," Carol said, laughing at her joke as Ivy rolled her eyes.

"You are lovely, Carol. And your body is really nice," Ivy said, surprising Carol as she felt her hand on her thigh.

"Really nice?" Carol teased, making Ivy bite her bottom lip.

"Yeah, it feels safe. Like a Mommy or whatever," Ivy replied, beginning to blush. Carol noticed that whenever Ivy spoke from her heart, she would finish the sentence with the word whatever to try and create some emotional distance.

It must have been so rough for you, little girl, Carol thought to herself thinking, having involuntarily placed her hand on top of Ivy's.

"Well, there's plenty of time for that later. Right now, let's get this little tummy filled," Carol said, pulling into the restaurant and tickling Ivy as they walked inside.

"Ok, this is amazing!" Ivy exclaimed, looking around at the three leveled building and the huge buffets on each level. Carol directed her to a secluded table and sat next to Ivy.

"I like that you sat there, it makes it feel less like an interview or whatever," Ivy said as Carol put her arm around her.

"Can I do this?" Carol asked, Ivy, pulling away from her slightly.

"Yeah. It makes me feel a bit weird though," Ivy replied, as Carol nodded and took her arm away.

"But I like it," Ivy quickly added, taking Carol's arm and wrapping it back around her, making Carol laugh.

"Alright," she said, squeezing Ivy firmly.

After 2 hours at the restaurant, Ivy was finally full.

"I have no idea where all that food goes!" Carol teased. She thought it was cute that Ivy had a full little tummy, happy that she was able to give the girl what she wanted.

"This was great. I don't think I will move for a month, but so worth it," Ivy replied, resting into Carol. Carol noticed how Ivy's eyes began to look over her, and she laughed.

"I don't think I can tonight, honey. I'm not like you, if I eat a big meal, that's me done for the night," Carol explained.

"But you could watch me and tell me what to do," Ivy seductively whispered into Carol's ear, making her pussy instantly tingle.

"Careful what you wish for young lady," Carol said, patting Ivy's thigh predatorily.

"Come on, let's get out of here," Ivy said, kissing Carol on the cheek. Carol felt such a strong urge to tell Ivy that she was a Mommy Dom, but she was afraid that Ivy would freak out and end their time together, so she decided that she would try to put it into the game Ivy wanted to play. Carol began to drive out of the lot as she saw Ivy start to tear at her cuticles.

"Pull your dress up," Carol instructed, taking Ivy by surprise. Ivy looked up at Carol and, without breaking eye contact, slowly lifted the hem of her dress high enough that Carol could see her pink lace panties through her tights.

"Spread your thighs for me," Carol continued, her voice becoming hoarse with desire. Ivy slowly obeyed, pushing herself forward and feeling her clit begin to throb.

"Like this?" Ivy replied, pushing her pussy out and arching her back.

"Just like that," Carol replied, reaching down to stroke her over her tights. Feeling the heat coming from Ivy's sex, Carol pulled on her tights, and in one quick motion, her hand was in Ivy's panties. Feeling Ivy's wetness, Carol tenderly stroked Ivy's slit, pushing her pussy lips apart and teasing her hole.

"Such a sweet little thing," Carol purred, having to remind herself that she was driving and to stay focused.

"Play with your titties for me," Carol instructed, feeling her own clit begin to pulse and swell as she watched Ivy follow her commands. Carol pulled on Ivy's puffy pussy lips allowing her juices to coat her fingers before Carol flicked her wrist and was inside of Ivy before her body knew what was happening.

"Oh my god," Ivy gasped, sitting up quickly as she felt Carol's fingers inside of her.

"Just tell me red if you want me to stop, alright?" Carol lovingly said as she began to wriggle her fingers inside of Ivy. They pulled into the motel car park, and Carol turned off the engine.

"Kiss me," Carol instructed, smiling into the kiss as she felt Ivy's tongue against hers as she unbuckled her seat belt. Carol continued to finger fuck Ivy, reaching over and pushing her chair back and climbing on top of her. She liked that Ivy still had her seat belt on. It made Carol feel even more dominating as she saw Ivy's restricted body.

"Stick your tongue out for me," Carol said breathlessly as she unbuttoned her blouse with her other hand, her body lying gently on top of Ivy's.

"Suck my nipple," Carol instructed, moaning loudly in pure delight as she felt Ivy suckle on her desperately.

"Yes, baby girl," Carol groaned as she fucked her slowly. Carol didn't want Ivy over the edge just yet, and she kept her a writhing mess under her as she pleasured her.

"Say, I like it, Mommy," Carol moaned involuntarily, Ivy almost freezing underneath her. Ivy pushed Carol's heavy breast from her lips.

"Mommy, I like it," came the words Carol longed to hear, putting her breast back in Ivy's mouth and fucking her harder.

"That's it, baby girl," Carol moaned as she felt Ivy's pussy relax and her eyes roll to the back of her head.

Why do I like this? What the fuck?! Ivy yelled to herself, but any other thoughts where fucked from her mind as Carol took her over the edge, making her squirt for the first time. Ivy looked up at Carol, who bent her head to kiss her on the tip of her nose, frowning as she saw Ivy's eyes begin to swell.

"Honey, what is it?" Carol lovingly asked. Getting off Ivy, Carol moved back to her seat as Ivy wiped the tears from her eyes.

"Nothing. Sorry," Ivy replied, getting out the car and walking toward her door.

"Hey, it's not nothing. Talk to me, honey," Carol said, getting out and following Ivy into her room. Ivy was sitting on the bed as Carol walked in and shut the door. Ivy looked up at her as tears streamed down her face.

She is a beautiful crier, Carol thought, sitting next to Ivy and putting her hand on the girl's thigh.

"Baby girl?" Carol questioned as Ivy got up and began to pace around the small room.

"I don't know. I don't know why I am crying or what I'm doing, and this all just feels like so much," Ivy said, beginning to hyperventilate. Carol got up and walked over to her, took her hand, and led her back to the bed.

Carol positioned Ivy, so she was being cradled, and as Ivy pushed her away, Carol just held on tighter.

"Just wait, sweetheart. I'm not going to hurt you. You're safe with me. Let me soothe that hurt in your heart, darling," Carol affectionately said, gently rocking Ivy in her arms, feeling the girl relax but maintain her furrowed expression.

"I don't know how to handle all this," Ivy whispered as Carol thumbed away her endless tears rolling down her face.

"I know, honey. Is it because I'm so loving?" Carol asked, making Ivy bite her bottom lip.

"Maybe," Ivy replied, turning into Carol and burying her face into the older woman's cleavage.

"Why did you want me to, you know, call you Mommy?" Ivy shyly said, her words muffled against Carol's shirt. Carol felt a knot begin to tighten in her stomach, hoping that this wasn't the night she would lose Ivy. Carol took a deep breath and exhaled slowly, Ivy sensing there was something to this story and getting up to sit next to Carol.

"So, have you heard of BDSM before?" Carol asked Ivy, who just rolled her eyes, making Carol laugh.

"Like everyone has," Ivy replied, happy with herself that she knew what it was.

"Well, there are different types of expressing those core elements and values of BDSM, in particular, D and s. One of those ways is for the Dom to express themselves in a more nurturing and almost maternal if you like, method of dominating their submissive. Then, in turn, the submissive enjoys that type of domination, where they are looked after and cared for as though they are younger than they biologically are," Carol said, trying to explain MDLG as best she could, laughing as Ivy tilted her head as she listened.

"Ok, so it's like a lot less whips and orgasm denial and more, like what?" Ivy replied,

Carol, finding it endearing that Ivy wanted to share all her knowledge.

"Well, like everything in BDSM, both parties need to agree on how their relationship will be. But for me, I like it when the submissive calls me Mommy. And I like calling my sub pet names like baby girl, little one, and just generally sweet names that a Mommy would call her baby. I like looking after my girl, but I enjoy that to be from a more maternal slant than anything else," Carol said, realizing that she had never had to explain MDLG to someone before. Usually, she wouldn't bother getting involved with a girl who didn't identify as an AB, but she couldn't pull herself from Ivy, no matter how hard she had tried.

"Ok. So, wow, that's kinda interesting, I guess," Ivy said, trying to find a place to process that information.

"So, what stuff would you do then?" Ivy questioned, getting up and walking over to where her water bottle sat.

"Honestly, it would depend on what was agreed upon. Usually, people who enjoy this kink enjoy doing things called 'little things.' It depends on how they feel. They might feel like they want to be cared for like a baby, and then they want their food to be cut up and to play with soft toys and have naps, for example. But then on the other end, you have what is called 'middles' who are a lot more independent because they feel like they want to be cared for still but also have a lot more desire to be independent. If you want, I can send you some really good content to explain it more," Carol explained, Ivy finding the conversation interesting.

"So, it's like, a lifestyle thing or a sex thing?" She asked, coming to sit back down next to Carol.

"It could be one or the other, or it could be both. It just depends on the type of dynamic between the two people," Carol said, watching as Ivy took in all the new information.

"Cool," Ivy suddenly said, shrugging her

shoulders, making Carol laugh.

"Cool?" She questioned, wanting a little more insight into what Ivy was thinking.

"Yeah, so like, you're a Mommy Dom, so what?" Ivy said, crossing her legs and looking up at Ivy.

"Right, and for this to continue then, you'd have to enjoy being my little or middle, I'm not really fussed which one, I adore both," Carol said, watching the penny drop for Ivy.

"Oh. Ok, I don't know what you'd want me to do," Ivy replied, making Carol laugh.

"How about this. You take a week or so and spend some time researching the kink and see if it's something that resonates with you. If it doesn't, that is totally fine. You'll never lose me as a friend, but we shouldn't continue to see each other in this capacity because it wouldn't be fair on either of us," Carol explained, sweeping Ivy's hair out of her eyes.

"Yeah, there's nothing worse than not meshing with someone," Ivy replied, kissing

Carol on the cheek.

"Ok, get out. I have to search the hell out of this stuff," Ivy playfully said, pushing Carol off the bed.

"Alright, alright!" Carol exclaimed, giving in and getting up. She turned around and found Ivy on her knees on the bed, reaching out for a hug at which Carol rolled her eyes.

"You kick me out, then want cuddles? Such a baby," Carol playfully said as she held onto Ivy before kissing her goodnight.

Chapter 4

Ivy didn't sleep for two nights after Carol left. Between working at the diner and researching everything she could on ABDL and MDLG, she didn't have time for anything else, least of all sleep. Carol had messaged her a few links to different websites, but the thank you messages was all she had heard of Ivy. Carol was wondering by the third week of silence what Ivy was up to and decided to give her a call, frowning when she didn't pick up.

Damn, I might have scared her off. That was the last thing I wanted to do. Maybe I should call her and see if she's free for dinner or something, Carol thought to herself as she sipped wine at a bar with her work colleagues.

"Your turn!" Hope exclaimed as Carol felt her thigh being shaken and looked around at the girls' faces in front of her, their expectant and expressive faces telling her that she must have missed something.

"Sorry I was somewhere else. What?" Carol said, making the girls' laugh.

"Oh, we know, you've been somewhere else all week!" Gabi exclaimed, making Carol roll her eyes.

"So, the question was, where have you had public sex?" Hope questioned, sipping her drink and smirking. Carol had slept with Hope when she first came to the practice. It was nothing particularly noteworthy and very vanilla, but Hope had clearly enjoyed her time. Carol raised an eyebrow.

Why don't you tell them, honey? Carol said to herself as she stared Hope down, making her blush and quickly look away.

"In the back seat of my car, in a parking lot at the beach at midnight," Carol replied, with wicked satisfaction that Hope excused herself to go to the bathroom. Gabi just laughed and clapped her hands as Carol chuckled to herself.

"Oh, you girls. I have had a lovely time, but I must go," Carol said as soon as Hope returned.

"But you've only had one drink!" Gabi said, enjoying how Carol looked at her and put her back in her place.

"I'll see you two on Monday. Try not to break too many hearts between now and then," Carol said, standing up and putting her coat on, winking at them before she left the bar. Walking down the street, Carol took her phone out, dialing Ivy's number but deciding not to call her and put her phone back into her coat pocket in frustration.

Fuck it, Carol thought hailing a taxi and deciding to go to Ivy's motel room.

Ivy had worked a double shift, and she wearily dragged her feet down the street. She knew what she wanted to do the moment she got home, have a bath, and snuggle into her blankets. Tonight was going to be her last night in the motel as she had successfully acquired a small unit to rent closer to town. She turned the corner of the last block she had to walk and thought about how nice it would be to have a fluffy onesie to wear to bed. Biting her lip and wondering how long it would take her to afford half of the little things she had decided she needed. Ivy had decided that she definitely had some of the interests of a little and had experimented with getting into little space, realizing that is was considerably harder to do without Carol around. But she also wanted to explore it without Carol around because she was embarrassed about the thought of being in that space and doing the things she wanted to do with Carol watching her. So she had decided to just hide from Carol, which had been working well until she looked up to see Carol out the front of her motel room.

"Hi," Carol said as she saw Ivy stop walking and stand half frozen. Ivy looked around, unable to hide any longer.

"Hey," she replied, fumbling in her

backpack for her keys. Carol watched, wanting to have this conversation but also not wanting to make Ivy run.

"I haven't heard from you," Carol said as Ivy stood in the doorway. Ivy just shrugged her shoulders, looking up at Carol and raised her eyebrows in the bratty way that Carol loved.

"Ok," Carol decisively said, walking into the motel room and pushing Ivy aside before sitting on the edge of the bed.

"Hey, you can't just barge in here," Ivy complained, Carol just shrugging her shoulders and gave Ivy the same look she was just graced with.

"Fuck, what do you want from me?" Ivy angrily replied, annoyed that she couldn't understand the feelings she was feeling.

"I want you to try to tell me what's going on," Carol lovingly said, disarming Ivy and making her less angry and combative.

"I don't know the words," Ivy softly said as she felt her heart soften and begin to hurt. Ivy had gotten used to being on her own. She had gotten somewhat comfortable with having no one to rely on, and she had made peace with the fact that no one cared about her. And then Carol had come along and changed all of that, and it was just too much for her to feel. Too different, too loving and too kind.

"I've never had somebody care. I don't know what it's meant to feel like. When you are nice to me, it like, hurts," Ivy tried to explain, Carol nodding her head and wincing as she imagined how much pain Ivy must continuously feel. Carol took her coat off, deciding that she wasn't going anywhere tonight.

"Baby," she said affectionately and reached out her hand to Ivy. Ivy looked at her with hesitant eyes, wanting to be embraced but also wanting to feel the familiar feeling of neglect.

"You smell good, Mommy," Ivy mumbled into Carol's neck, making Carol gasp and hold onto Ivy firmer, not wanting to let you go.

"I've missed you," Ivy confessed, looking up at Carol and hoping that the older woman would never leave her.

"I know darling, I've missed you too," Carol said, kissing Ivy on the forehead and rocking her in her arms. They stayed like that, Carol nurturing Ivy as the night dragged on. Carol had underestimated how invested she had become in Ivy and felt herself going into Mommy space quickly and more deeply than she had experienced. It wasn't the frenzied obsession she had experienced during their first dates. It was something deeper, something calm and powerful, a feeling of primal protection and lust and desire that caused a gleam of passion to reflect in her eyes. Ivy noticed the change and rolled out of Carol's embrace, standing up in front of her.

"Can I show you something?" Ivy asked, Carol, smiling at her lovingly, the warmth in her eyes pulling Ivy into her little space, making her giggle. Ivy looked at Carol with a disarming look,

Carol hadn't seen too frequently, and she sighed in contented bliss as she felt the world turn in slow motion.

"Of course, honey," Carol replied, watching as Ivy crouched down next to the bed and took out a box, opening the lid and stepping back. Carol looked at Ivy, who began to blush as Carol peered inside. She raised an eyebrow as she saw the contents, before smiling up at Ivy.

"Well, you have been busy," Carol said, patting her lap, delighted that Ivy walked over to her without thinking about it and sat on her lap as they looked into the box together.

"I researched," Ivy proudly said as she reached in and took out a pink paci.

"Mm, I see that," Carol replied, taking it from Ivy's hand and teasing her mouth open with it. Carol felt her heart pounding as Ivy rested her head back on Carol's shoulder as she sucked her paci, playing with Carol's long hair as she snuggled.

"What else do you have in here,

sweetheart?" Carol asked, taking out a diaper and watching as Ivy's eyes grew wide, and she snapped out of little space, taking the paci from her lips.

"Um, I haven't tried that yet," Ivy said, her adult voice filled with the usual fear Carol had become accustomed too.

"And we don't have to, baby," Carol said, easing Ivy's fears.

"Ok, cool," Ivy said, the silence between her and Carol almost deafening.

"So, would you interested in putting that back in your little mouth and letting me get you out of these work clothes?" Carol asked, wanting her sweet little girl back in her arms. Ivy thought for a moment before biting her lip and putting her paci back in, Carol's encouraging smile easing her nerves.

"Have you eaten, baby?" Carol asked as she slowly undressed Ivy, seeing her protruding ribs. Carol frowned, noticing that Ivy was skinnier than usual. Ivy just shook her head and laughed when Carol rolled her eyes.

"I can just make a sandwich," Ivy said, lifting her legs up so Carol could take off her ripped skinny jeans.

"Hmm, let me do it while you shower," Carol said, holding Ivy lovingly before she walked back out to the table Ivy had been using as a kitchen bench.

I need to get her out of here, Carol thought as she made Ivy a peanut butter sandwich. Ivy walked out of the shower, naked and wrapped her arms around Carol, taking a bite of the sandwich.

"Get a plate, you little monster," Carol laughed.

"I don't have any plates," Ivy quickly replied, giggling as Carol rolled her eyes and grabbed the diaper in one hand, and she held onto Ivy's waist with the other. Carol raised a questioning eyebrow at Ivy, who just swallowed a mouthful of sandwich in a gulp before nodding her head slowly.

"Lay up on the bed for Mommy," Carol loving instructed, Ivy, feeling her cheeks flush pink.

"It's ok, baby. Mommy needs to get you ready for bed," Carol said, stroking Ivy's forehead until she relaxed.

"We can stop whenever you want, baby," Carol whispered as she kissed Ivy's cheek and stayed pressing her body into Ivy's as she wrapped her arms around Carol's neck. Slowly releasing her, Ivy opened her mouth and let Carol put her paci into her mouth. Carol slid the diaper under Ivy's bottom and tenderly ran her fingers over the girl's body before fastening the diaper to her waist. Seeing the slight embarrassment creep back into Ivy's eyes, Carol quickly pulled on Ivy's pajama bottoms and a baggy t-shirt, as Ivy grabbed at her.

"Alright, alright, baby, do you want to cuddle with Mommy?" Carol laughed as Ivy became slightly frantic in her need to be snuggled into Carol's deep cleavage. Nodding,

Ivy curled up into Carol, her sleepy eyes making
Carol turn the lights off in the room and feeling
Ivy's breathing become slow, kissed her baby girl
goodnight.

Chapter 5

"I've heard some people get really non-verbal when they are in little space," Ivy said the moment Carol opened her eyes the next morning. Blinking, Carol looked around the room and let herself adjust to being awake.

"Pardon?" Carol sleepily asked, wondering how late it was, the sun was streaming through the windows, and she guessed that it was no wonder that Ivy never slept in with how bright the room became.

"Some littles become non-verbal when they are in little space," Ivy repeated as though she had just discovered something nobody else knew.

"Yes. What is your point, baby?" Carol said, sitting up and watching as Ivy's eyes lit up.

"I think I am one of those. Because last night when I was sleepy and deep in little space,

I didn't want to talk," Ivy explained, feeling empowered as she understood something about herself for the first time. Carol smiled and pulled her into her arms.

"Well, that would definitely explain your little grabby hands, baby girl," Carol said playfully, covering Ivy's face in kisses.

"So, you do have work today?" Carol asked, watching Ivy play with her breasts.

"Nope, I am moving into my new place today!" Ivy exclaimed, Carol, tilting her head in curiosity.

"Really? Where are you moving to?" Carol asked, putting her bra on much to Ivy's disappointment.

"It's like ten minutes' walk to the middle of town," Ivy replied, sitting up on the bed and feeling the diaper crinkle into her, reminding her that she was wearing one. Carol noticed the shock on her face, unsure of which space to be in as the new day dawned.

"Well, that sounds like you have a lot of

big girl things to do. Do you want Mommy to take your diaper off so you can put your big girl panties on, darling?" Carol asked, Ivy, pulling her usual thinking face before nodding her head.

"Say, yes, please, Mommy," Carol lovingly prompted, enjoying gently training her baby girl.

"Yes, please, Mommy," Ivy repeated, looking down and touching the front of her diaper. Carol liked that Ivy was so sweet and unguarded when she was in little space and wondered if she would get to the stage where she was comfortable wetting her diaper.

"Ok, lay down for Mommy," Carol said, moving so she was crouching down next to Ivy. Ivy let Carol put her paci in her mouth as she took the diaper off and pulled on Ivy's panties. Ivy wriggling playfully as Carol's hair tickled her tummy.

"Oh, you are just too precious," Carol said, sitting back and looking at her sweet girl.

"So, like what are we?" Ivy asked, resting on her elbows, her paci in her hand.

"What would you like to be? Do you want this to be labeled?" Carol asked, excited that Ivy wanted to commit to her.

"Yeah, like, are we together or just like, I don't know, fucking around?" Ivy asked, trying to explain her thinking, making Carol laugh as she playfully spanked Ivy's ass.

"Hey!" Ivy exclaimed, nuzzling into Carol as she wrapped her arms around her.

"You're funny. We are not fucking around. I would like this to continue, do you want me to ask you if you want to be my girlfriend?" Carol asked, amused that she was having this conversation. Usually, when she was with a girl, she never used terms like girlfriend, but as she eased Ivy into the kink, she felt it wouldn't go astray to make connections that Ivy understood.

"Yep," Ivy simply replied. Carol stood up and put her blouse back on. Ivy's eyes never leaving her.

"Do you want to be my girlfriend, Ivy?" Carol asked, pulling her trousers on and watching Ivy's eyes light up.

"Yes, very much so," Ivy replied, getting on her knees from the bed and cuddling Carol's waist, snuggling into her and feeling safe for the first time in a long time.

"Well, good. And you're happy to keep learning about MDLG? You aren't going to lose me if you don't," Carol asked, not wanting to have Ivy be with her but not enjoy the kink.

"Mommy," Ivy said, giving Carol a playful look.

"You might have introduced me to the whole thing, but I'm the one who learned that I liked it," Ivy said, putting all of Carol's fears aside. Ivy reached for Carol's blouse, and slowly unbuttoned the buttons Carol had just done up.

"What do you think you're doing?" Carol asked as Ivy pulled it off and threw it on the bed.

"What does it look like I'm doing," Ivy said, pulling her top off and moving closer to Carol. Carol smirked and grabbed Ivy's hair, turning her around and pushing her down until she was on all fours on the bed. Carol gripped Ivy's hips in her hands and pushed against her ass making her giggle.

"Mommy," Ivy half whined, turning Carol on as she dry humped Ivy's ass.

"You know, little girls who tease Mommy, always get themselves in far deeper than they thought they would," Carol said, reaching around and pushing her hand into Ivy's jeans, cupping her panty covered pussy. Ivy gasped and arched her back as she felt Carol pull her panties to the side and push her head down.

"You're lucky I don't have my strap on here, or this little pussy would be destroyed," Carol said as she began to fuck Ivy at a pace she wanted. Ivy moaned and gripped the sheets, her back muscles flexing and straining as she let Carol pound into her.

"Mommy, I," Ivy started to beg just as she tightened her pussy muscles and relaxed, feeling her cunt flood and her hips drop. Carol wasn't finished and lay on top of Ivy as she continued to take her, loving how the girl was panting and moaning as another orgasm shook her little body.

"Sure a good girl," Carol cooed as she pulled out from Ivy and cuddled her affectionately. Ivy just sucked her thumb and snuggled into Carol, beaming up at her.

"Don't you have any furniture?" Carol asked Ivy as they took her backpack and travel bag into the new place. Ivy was busy walking around the space, in heaven that this was all hers.

"Um, no," Ivy replied. She planned to just sleep on the floor until she could afford a bed and take it from there.

"So no fridge, no washing machine or dryer, no bed or cupboard," Carol said, looking at Ivy and smiling at how impressed Ivy looked.

"Yep. But it's got a really soft carpet and a modern kitchen and bathroom, and I can actually afford it!" Ivy replied, warming Carol's heart.

"Ok, princess. Come on. Mommy is about to get her Mommy on," Carol said, watching as Ivy tilted her head to the side, trying to understand what Carol meant. Happily skipping over to where she was standing, Ivy held Carol's extended hand and walked out the door.

"Where are we going?" Ivy asked, her stomach rumbling making Carol laugh.

"First, we are getting breakfast, then I am buying you furniture for your new place," Carol explained, confusing Ivy.

"Why?" Ivy asked, surprised that Carol would suggest such a big gesture.

"What do you mean, why?! You haven't got a bed, darling," Carol said, pointing out the obvious, not making Ivy any less confused.

"But you don't need to do any of that stuff. Maybe breakfast. But you don't need to buy me other things," Ivy explained, Carol rolling her eyes as they stopped at a trendy breakfast bar.

"Baby girl. Mommy isn't just your

girlfriend, and this isn't an equal thing for me, where we only do things that we can both afford or do. This is a; I look after you to the absolute best of my ability and capacity, sort of thing. Like what a sugar Mommy would do, but I don't expect you to fuck me in return. I know you are a big independent girl who doesn't need anyone, but Mommy wants to look after you. I want to make sure you have a big comfy bed to sleep in, that you have a fridge to put all your snacks in and help you make a nice home so that when Mommy isn't with you, I know you are in a safe space with everything you could need. Maybe also a few things you want," Carol explained, enjoying watching Ivy take in all the information.

"So, like, somebody I can count on all the time?" Ivy softly asked, having the painful feeling in her heart as the fear that Carol might end up leaving her racked her mind. Carol nodded, wiping the tear that escaped Ivy's eyes and kissing the tip of her nose.

"But what if you go?" Ivy whispered. Carol

got out of her SUV and walked around to Ivy's side, opening the door and unbuckling her seatbelt.

"If I ever was to go, it would be because it would be best for both of us. And I wouldn't just abandon you, baby girl. I would make sure you were alright and taken care of and supported. Mommy wouldn't just up and go and not tell you why alright? So you don't need to worry yourself with that thought because I have no intention of leaving you," Carol said, holding onto Ivy and gently pulling her from her seat until she was standing up.

"Ok," Ivy said, wiping her tears away and nodding her head, deciding to believe Carol.

"Good," Carol replied, taking Ivy's hand and walking into the restaurant with Ivy's hand firmly holding hers.

"Tell me what you like," Carol said as they walked into the furniture store. Carol made Ivy write a list of all the things she needed and thought it was sweet that Ivy was surprised with the items Carol insisted on buying her.

"I really don't think I need shoe racks," Ivy laughed as Carol put two into the trolley.

"Where are you planning on storing your shoes then?" Carol asked, an eyebrow raised.

"Like, on the floor," Ivy said, shrugging her shoulder, Carol nodding to herself, satisfied that Ivy needed them after her response. Ivy just laughed and followed Carol around the store.
They picked out a bed, a cupboard, and a fridge, Ivy putting in pink bunny bed linen and making Carol smirk.

"Such a baby girl," she whispered as she also put in plain white and navy sets.

"For when you don't feel little. It's important to honor all the sides of yourself," Carol explained as Ivy started to take them out of the trolley, just to think for a moment and put them back down.

"Makes sense. It's really easy to get sucked into that place and never want to leave. But I guess sometimes I'll have to, huh?" Ivy asked, putting in pillows and fluffy blankets.

"Exactly," Carol replied, adding bath towels to the trolley. They ended up also buying a two-seater sofa, a coffee table, tv cabinet, two rugs, a tv, microwave, crockery, cooking utensils, cutlery, and a house plant. Ivy had won the battle of the washing machine as she said she would rather use a laundromat because it is fun. Carol seriously doubted how much fun waiting for laundry would be, but as Ivy was adamant she liked to use them, Carol made Ivy agree to tell her when going wasn't fun anymore and that she would get her one for her place then. They had decided to get everything delivered that afternoon, and as Carol drove Ivy to an ice-cream parlor, Ivy's head was spinning.

"I'm so grateful. I'm so surprised, I'm so like, wow," Ivy said, her mind racing with what had just happened. Never in her life had anyone ever bought her something, and then this amazingly beautiful woman not only wanted to be in her life, but she also was totally fine with spending thousands of dollars on her just to make sure she had cool stuff.

"Are you happy?" Carol asked, already knowing the answer. Ivy just looked at her with wide, surprised eyes and nodded yes.

"So happy, Mommy," Ivy said, holding Carol's hand as she drove.

Chapter 6

"How will you get to work, baby girl?" Carol asked as she woke up in Ivy's new bed Sunday morning. Carol had made sure that Ivy was settled into her new place, but had secretly not been able to bear the thought of leaving her alone. She wanted to be in Mommy space with Ivy for as long as she could, and Ivy never seemed to mind.

"I'm catching the bus, but I am working the late shift, so we have until 4," Ivy replied from the bathroom. She had woken up early and gone to have a shower.

"I don't know how I feel about you working the night shift," Carol said, walking into the bathroom as Ivy dried herself.

"Why? Are you scared something might happen to me?" Ivy teased, Carol grabbing her wrist and pulling her into her.

"Maybe," Carol replied, swaying with Ivy making her giggle.

"Well, don't be. Hardly anyone comes into the diner past midnight anyway. Plus, the pay is a little better working night shifts," Ivy replied, making Carol raise an eyebrow.

"Are you busy today? Do you want to do something?" Ivy asked Carol, escaping her grip and running into the bedroom. Carol lay on the bed as she watched Ivy dress. She pulled on her signature black skinny jeans and baggy band t-shirt and tied her hair up in a messy ponytail.

"What?" Ivy asked as she saw the subtle smile spread over Carol's lips.

"You are just so perfect," Carol replied, making Ivy blush.

"Yes, let's do some grocery shopping," Carol replied, making Ivy roll her eyes.

"Mommy, that's so boring," Ivy whined, making Carol laugh. Usually, she had a no whining policy, but she and Ivy hadn't talked about rules or punishments, and Carol was hoping to keep that conversation for a later time. She was worried that Ivy would be triggered and emotionally withdraw from her if the topic of punishments came up, and Carol didn't want that to happen.

"I know it is, but we can make it fun. Is your food budget still meal by meal? Maybe we need to start thinking about having a weekly food budget instead so that you always have food around and don't have to worry about being hungry," Carol suggested.

"Oh, I'm never worried when I'm hungry," Ivy playfully teased.

"You are such a cheeky girl," Carol replied, taking Ivy's hand and heading out the door.

"What is the point of this stuff?" Ivy asked as Carol put in tinned tomatoes into the trolley.

"Because I am going to teach you how to cook so that you don't keep buying sugary cereals and think that it is an appropriate snack," Carol replied, making Ivy laugh.

"But it has a nice crunch to it," Ivy replied, getting a playful spank on her ass. Carol bought the ingredients to make simple dishes like Bolognese, carbonara, and bacon and egg pie. Ivy tried to sneak in as much junk food as she could get away with, adding cakes and soda to the trolley just for Carol to take most of it out again.

"Choose three trash foods, and that is it, young lady," Carol said, holding Ivy's chin in her hand and making her look up at her until she blushed. Ivy hadn't heard Carol's strict Mommy voice before, and it made her excited, slightly turned on, but also aware that she didn't want to piss Carol off. Ivy chose a packet of chips, a bag of gummy bears, and a tub of ice-cream in no time at all, coming to the register and taking out her purse.

"It's ok, baby," Carol softly said, Ivy's eyes going wide.

"What do you mean?" She whispered back as the lady scanned the groceries.

"Let me set you up, you can buy them for yourself next time," Carol replied, paying the lady and walking out of the store, Ivy numbly following behind her.

"Why are you doing all this nice stuff for me?" Ivy asked on the way back to her apartment. Carol placed her hand on Ivy's thigh and rubbed it affectionately.

"Because I want to, if I'm selfish, it makes me feel good to look after you. You deserve somebody who can treat you right, and I want that person to be me. This is what I meant when I said that I view my role in the relationship as the person to take care of you. I don't expect you to take care of me like this, because that isn't what a baby is meant to do; it's Mommy's job. I expect different things from you," Carol replied, Ivy, listening attentively.

"Like what?" Ivy asked, her little voice escaping her, making her laugh.

"I expect that you are loyal to me," Carol began to say, making Ivy laugh.

"That's kinda like the most basic rule of being in a monogamous relationship," she said, making Carol smile. She didn't like being interrupted, but she would let that one slide.

"I expect you to be honest with me. If we do something that you are uncomfortable with, I expect that you tell me straight away. I will push a little bit on your limits, but if you ever feel that it's too much, you need to tell me. It's not tough to push way past what you are comfortable with, even if it's not a physical thing, emotion and psychological boundaries need to be respected by you and by me. And most of the time, I will be able to read who you feel, but you still need to tell me, alright," Carol explained. Ivy listened as she watched Carol pull up at her apartment.

"Yeah, that all makes sense," Ivy said, taking two shopping bags in her hands and walking inside.

"That all sounds really heavy and serious," Ivy said as she began to put the groceries away. Carol placed her hands on Ivy's shoulders and turned her around.

"It is," she replied, smiling down at Ivy, putting her at ease.

"What else? I know that can't be it. I've read things online about rules and stuff," Ivy said, taking out a bottle of water and sitting on the sofa, Carol coming to join her.

"Oh, have you now?" She teased, pulling Ivy into her arms, making her snuggle into her chest.

"Yep," Ivy said, closing her eyes as she listened to Carol's heartbeat.

"I don't want to give you so much to think about just yet. Let's start with you calling me Mommy. Not when you are in front of your friends or at work, but every other time," Carol said as Ivy sipped the water.

"And, how would you feel about wearing a diaper to bed and letting me pick out your pajamas?" Carol asked Ivy as she kissed the top of her head.

"Ok, Mommy," Ivy said, nuzzling into

Carol. The warmth of her body made Ivy sleepy, and Carol checked the time to make sure she wouldn't be late for work.

"Come on, little girl. No time for naps on Mommy right now. You need to get ready for work," Carol said, gently pulling Ivy off her chest.

"But, Mommy," Ivy softly whined, her grabby hands reaching out for Carol.

"How about this. Mommy will pick you up in the morning before I go to woke and make sure you get home safely and all cleaned up and tucked into bed?" Carol suggested. Looking into Ivy's yearning gaze, she knew that she and Ivy would need to find a way to have a compatible work schedules.

She needs me, Carol thought as Ivy put her thumb in her mouth and nodded her head.

"Alright. Come on, let me get you ready for work then," Carol said, taking Ivy's thumb from her lips and replacing it with her paci. Carol walked over to Ivy's new cupboard, took out her uniform and lingerie, and returned to the bed.

Taking Ivy's arms, she undressed her until she was lying naked on the bed. Carol admired the girl's youthful body, feeling her pussy begin to tingle and moisten.

"You are so beautiful," Carol said as she stroked Ivy's body from her collar bone to her clit, making Ivy squirm and giggle.

"Mommy," Ivy said playfully and jumped into Carol's loving arms. Ivy loved the feeling of Carol's arm completely enclosing her body, and she snuggled into the nook of Carol's neck as she closed her eyes once more. Feeling her body become heavy, Carol stood up and let Ivy gently fall on the bed, smiling at her warmly when she opened her eyes.

"Give Mommy your paci baby girl. You don't need that anymore," Carol said, as Ivy obeyed her.

"Such a good girl," Carol added as she began to dress Ivy in her work uniform. Carol had chosen Ivy's black lace panties and matching bra and had to restrain herself from rubbing over

Ivy's nipples with her thumbs as she saw them become hard. Ivy noticed her cheeky sparkle in her eye, not going unnoticed by Carol.

"Do you like how it looks, Mommy?" Ivy teased, getting to her knees and rubbing her hands over her perky breasts. Carol just glared at Ivy before turning around to take her uniform in her hands. She raised an eyebrow as she held it out to Ivy, who had begun to rub herself through her panties.

"Ivy," Carol warned, the stern tone in her voice making Ivy giggle as she continued to tease Carol. Carol sat down on the bed and watched as Ivy performed for her, never changing her expression and enjoying how Ivy upped her teasing to try and get Carol to crack. She pulled her panties down and sucked her finger before sliding it up and down her slit, causing Carol to clench her cunt tightly as it began to throb once more.

If I had a cock, it would be rock hard right now, Carol thought as she shifted and pulled Ivy towards her until the girl was straddling Carol's soft thigh. Carol held Ivy's hips down and pushed her thigh up, pressing her panties into her pussy and making her gasp.

"Mommy, I'm going to be late," Ivy giggled as she tried to push Carol away.

"Oh, you think you can tease Mommy and just get away with it?" Came Carol's throaty reply. Ivy half froze, her wide eyes of surprise turning Carol on as she began to rock Ivy's hips back and forth, hardening the girl's clit.

"Mommy," Ivy gasped as she placed both her hands on Carol's shoulders, biting her bottom lip and moaning as she was taken.

"There's a good girl," Carol moaned when she felt Ivy's hips move to their own accord. Carol unzipped her jeans and put her hand in her pants, enjoying watching Ivy get herself off in front of her. Carol held onto Ivy with one hand on her back as she rubbed her clit with the other. She tilted her head back as she felt her orgasm building inside of her and closed her eyes, and she lifted her thigh once more to have Ivy's pussy closer to hers.

"Tell Mommy when you are close, little bunny," Carol said as she felt her pussy explode, her squirting cunt soaking her panties and the crotch of her jeans. She watched as Ivy continued to jerk her pussy against Carol's thigh, desperate but not able to cum. Carol thought for a moment before quickly flipping Ivy onto her back, pushing her hand away, and began rubbing her. Carol pinned Ivy's hands above her head with one hand and pushed her nipple into Ivy's mouth before going back to rubbing the girl's clit. Carol loved the sound and feeling of Ivy moaning against her breast and fucked her harder. She could see that Ivy couldn't cum with just her clit being stimulated and gently pushed a finger into Ivy's pussy, causing her to groan in pleasure and buck her hips.

"This is what you want, baby girl? Mommy inside of you, getting you off with her tit in your mouth. Mommy's dirty, little girl," Carol said, causing Ivy to be taken to a place she had never explored before. Carol eased another finger into Ivy and began fucking her harder, knocking her clit with her knuckles at every push. Feeling Ivy's pussy begin to tighten, Carol fucked her faster, curling her fingers inside Ivy and hitting her g-spot. She wrapped her arm around Ivy's head as she lowered her body onto the girl's as she fucked her with a predatory passion, as Ivy screamed and shook violently, falling silent after her orgasm racked her body. Carol felt Ivy's juices coat her fingers and enjoyed how her cunt dripped as Carol took her fingers out of the girl. Ivy lay on the bed, breathing heavily, as though she had just sprinted up a hill, and Carol replaced her breast with Ivy's paci. She wiped her down with a wet wipe and continued to dress her until she was in her uniform, still laying on the bed.

"Mommy," Ivy softly said, the need in her eyes matched by her little voice.

"Mommy's here, baby. I'm not going

anywhere," Carol replied, wrapping Ivy in her
arms and rocking her gently.

Chapter 7

Carol had pinned a teddy bear pin to Ivy's uniform and watched as she practically skipped inside to start her shift. Carol had ended up driving Ivy to work because she had missed her bus. Deciding that she would get Chinese take-out, Carol drove to her favorite restaurant, picked up her order, and drove home.

Oh, it is going to get really lonely here the longer I am with her, Carol said to herself as she sat down on the couch and checked her phone. She had been hoping that Ivy had messaged her, but after seeing the blank screen, settled in for a night of movie streaming before the workweek began.

Mommy, I miss you. Ivy's message woke Carol up. Looking around the dark living room, the only light coming from the tv screen, Carol fumbled around the couch looking for her phone. Smiling as she saw the message from Ivy, she looked at the time. It was only half an hour earlier than she was planning on getting up, so deciding to have a shower and get dressed, Carol made her way to the bathroom. She stripped off and threw her clothes in the wash basket before running the warm water. Feeling horny, Carol got out of the shower and went to her top drawer, taking out her dildo and walking back into the shower, she lifted one leg onto the lower nook. Designed originally for shampoo and conditioner, but having become a personal favorite for scratching an itch. Carol pushed the soft silicone cock into her pussy in one slow motion, sighing in relief as she felt the dildo fill her, pressing on her hilt. She moaned as she quickly fucked herself, thinking of Ivy sitting in front of her, watching as she pleased herself.

"Do you like watching Mommy?" Carol said out loud, thinking of Ivy's eyes sparkling up at her. Pumping the dildo in and out of her cunt,

Carol enjoyed feeling like a dirty older woman as she imagined sticking the dildo into Ivy's mouth and making her lick and suck her juices off as her eyes watered. Cumming hard, Carol pulled the cock from her cunt and let her juices flow, moaning, putting it back in, and bringing herself to a second orgasm before she cleaned herself and got out of the shower.

That should do it, she thought as she dried herself, imagining that Ivy wouldn't be in the mood after her shift. Carol dressed in her work uniform, wrapping her coat around her curvaceous body and running her fingers through her wavy hair, deciding to wear it down until she got to work.

I'm in the parking lot, baby girl, was the message she gave Ivy as she waited for her. She was five minutes late, and Carol thought that was unusual. Carol played a game on her phone as she waited. Ten minutes passed and then 15 minutes, making Carol slightly agitated. Ivy knew that Carol still had to make it to her work on time. Deciding to go in and drag her girl away, Carol locked her SUV and went inside.

"Hey, is Ivy still here?" She asked another waitress who just nodded and pointed to out the back.

"Thanks," Carol said, surprised the waitress was so forthcoming with the information. Carol walked toward the back, feeling her stomach tighten as she heard loud yelling coming from behind a door. Turning the door handle, Carol walked in to see Ivy sitting on an office chair, her boss sitting on the edge of the desk, pulling on his cock.

"Hey, what the fuck, you can't be here. Fuck off!" The man aggressively said, putting his dick away. Ivy turned around to see Carol standing behind her, Ivy's mascara stained cheeks was all she needed to know.

"Carol, I," Ivy began to say, stopping as Carol held out her hand and glaring at the man.

"Let's go," was all Carol said as Ivy scrambled to collect her things. Carol fought the urge to punch the man in the face. Her main concern was getting her baby girl out of the situation.

"I'm sorry I called you Carol, I'm sorry that all happened," Ivy began to say as Carol drove towards her apartment.

"Baby girl, it's ok. You can call me Carol when there are other people around, remember?" Carol lovingly said as she watched Ivy break down in tears.

"Almost home, little one," Carol gently said as she pulled into Ivy's street, parking out the front and ushering her inside, locking the door behind her.

"How much time do you have?" Ivy asked, wiping her tears. Carol smiled at her kindly.

"As much time as you need. I messaged the girls and told them I'd be in later," Carol replied, Ivy, giving her a sideward smile.

"Let's get you out of these clothes," Carol said, causing Ivy to flinch as she reached out to touch her upper arm.

"Hey, little one, Mommy isn't going to hurt you," Carol said, opening her arms and waiting for Ivy to walk into them cautiously.

"There's my good girl," Carol said as she walked Ivy to the bathroom, stripping her clothes off.

"He said that he would give me a raise if I sucked his cock," Ivy softly, suddenly said as Carol turned on the shower and began to lather her body in shower gel.

"Oh, baby girl. He is a pig. I'm sorry that he put you in that situation. Why didn't you just get up and walk away?" Carol asked, watching as Ivy took over.

"I don't know, it kinda all happened so fast. He knew I was a lesbian; it was just like, too much for my mind to respond to. I felt frozen," Ivy replied, getting out of the shower and being wrapped in a towel before Carol took her to her bedroom.

"Good thing, Mommy, came barging in," Carol said, taking out a thick diaper and fluffy pink onesie.

"Yeah, you're good at barging into places," Ivy replied, giggling and feeling herself begin to relax. Her hands were reaching out and grabbing for Carol.

"Shh, baby girl, Mommy is here," Carol said, replying to Ivy's clinginess. Ivy sucked on the paci Carol put in her mouth and lay still as Carol diapered her, making her diaper particularly thick with an extra, double thickness pad before fastening the tabs and dressing Ivy in the onesie.

"Mommy's little bunny," Carol lovingly said Ivy touched the front of her diaper, wondering why Carol had made it so thick. Her thighs were forced to stay slightly apart, and Carol picked her up and placed her on her hip, surprising Ivy.

"Yeah, Mommy still has a few tricks up her sleeve, baby girl," Carol said, impressed with herself as she pulled back the sheets on Ivy's bed and lay her gently down. Carol lay next to Ivy as she snuggled into her chest, getting gentle pats on her padded bottom until she was almost asleep.

"Mommy wants you to stay like that until I come back and change you when my day is over. I don't want you going back to that diner. Mommy will support you until you find a new job. But that place is out of bounds now, alright sugar?" Carol whispered to Ivy as Ivy nodded her head before falling asleep.

"See you soon, little girl," Carol said as she kissed Ivy on the forehead and left for work, messaging Ivy the new rules about the diner before she started to drive.

After she woke up in the late afternoon, Ivy happily stayed in little space. She watched some cartoons, followed the Bolognese recipe that Carol had written down for her, and ate a late lunch while coloring in.

I wish every day could be like this, Ivy thought as she pulled on her fluffy black socks before walking to the kitchen and taking out a packet of popcorn. She messaged Carol several times, happy that Carol always replied quickly, and before she knew it, it was 5:30, and Carol was on her way back to her.

Carol raced back to Ivy the moment her shift evened and noticed the strange way Ivy was behaving the moment she walked into her apartment.

"Baby, what are you doing?" She said, putting her bag down and going to the fridge to take out a beer.

"I have to go to the bathroom, Mommy, but you said to stay like this," Ivy replied, making Carol laugh. She eyed Ivy and decided that she was going to see how far she could be pushed.

"Well, then go, baby girl. You can still go without taking that off," Carol replied, patting the spot on the couch next to her.

"It hurts too much to sit, Mommy," Ivy said. Carol took a long drink before putting her beer down and getting down on the floor, pulling Ivy down with her.

"Sit in front of me, baby girl," Carol lovingly said, falling into Mommy space as though a switch was flicked on in her mind. She pulled Ivy's hips back into her and wrapped her legs around Ivy's, pulling them open. Carol placed her hand over the mound of Ivy's pussy and pressed into her, her other hand pressing on her bladder.

"Mommy," Ivy said, beginning to squirm, fighting Carol as not to wet her diaper.

"Wet your diaper for Mommy, baby girl. It will feel so much better," Carol whispered, enjoying how Ivy's head moving from side to side made her breasts shake.

"I can't Mommy," Ivy whispered back, Carol seeing the blush of red beginning to cover Ivy's face.

"Such a good girl. Come on, little one. Mommy is right here, try for Mommy, baby," Carol encouraged, feeling Ivy's diaper becoming warm but stopping when Ivy gasped and sat up straight, pushing against Carol.

"Where are you trying to go, baby? Mommy has you in her arms," Carol gently teased, pressing on Ivy's bladder firmer and feeling her surrendered to her request and wetting her diaper.

"There there, Mommy's got you," Carol said as Ivy began to cry.

"You don't like being a wet girl, do you, baby?" Carol said as Ivy bit her bottom lip and shook her head.

"Well, Mommy can fix that. Lay down," Carol instructed Ivy, following her command immediately. Ivy looked up at Carol with the puppy dog eyes, which always melted Carol's heart. Carol had learned that Ivy gave her those eyes when she was deep in her little space, wanting to be looked after, wanting to be safe, and have somebody to trust and knowing that she was that person for Ivy made her heart swell.

"Bottom up," Carol instructed, gently

tapping Ivy's thighs, smiling down at her when she obeyed. Carol took Ivy's diaper away, wiped her clean, and slid another diaper underneath her. Ivy didn't feel like talking; she felt sad. Sad that somebody had tried to take advantage of her, sad that she thought she would have probably done it if she didn't have Carol. Carol had made it perfectly clear that Ivy wasn't to be with anyone but her, and even though the thought of sucking her bosses dick grossed her out, she knew in her heart that even three months ago, with the carrot of extra money being on the table, she would have done it.

"What are you thinking about, little one," Carol asked. Ivy looked up at her suddenly and shrugged her shoulders.

"I just feel like being quiet tonight, Mommy," she softly said. Carol guessed that Ivy's withdrawn behavior was because of the situation she had walked in on, and she frowned.

"Baby girl. Mommy needs you to tell me what is going on so I can help you," Carol said as she clipped Ivy's onesie back up and lifted her into her arms. Ivy just rested her head on Carol's chest and sucked her thumb. She couldn't find the words to describe what she felt, so she just closed her eyes and felt her heart feel heavy.

"I just feel sad, Mommy," Ivy replied softly, and Carol knew not to try and push her for anything else.

"Alright, baby girl. Can Mommy take the lead tonight, then?" Carol asked. She hated that she would have to leave Ivy alone in her apartment eventually and thought about racing home to pack an overnight bag. Ivy felt the same way and sighed heavily.

"Mommy, I don't want you to go," she said, tugging on Carol's woolly sweater.

"I don't want to go either, baby girl," Carol whispered back.

"How about I fix you up something for dinner, and you come to my house for a few nights?" Carol suggested. Ivy apartment was 20minutes from Carol's, and it made more sense for Ivy to go to her apartment as Carol's work was only 10minutes from her home. Ivy held her tummy and looked up at Carol, wishing she could be the happy girl she knew Carol loved.

"I don't really feel like eating, Mommy," she said as she shrugged her shoulders. Carol looked at Ivy and saw just how little she was feeling tonight and smiled.

"Then you can just have a bottle. Come on, darling, let's pack you a bag. You can come and see where Mommy lives," Carol said as Ivy nodded her head.

Carol had packed all of Ivy's clothes, granted there weren't many adult clothes to choose from, but her collections of onesies were also packed.

"Mommy has diapers at her house, so you don't need to pack yours, baby," Carol said when Ivy handed her a pink diaper.

"But do you have pink ones?" Ivy said, before putting her paci in her mouth. Carol smirked, kissed Ivy on the cheek, and packed the pink diapers.

"I think that is it, honey. Mommy has a special surprise for you in the car," Carol said, looking over the apartment one last time before closing the door. She had pulled a pair of baggy jeans over the top of Ivy's onesie and was happy to see how padded her bottom looked. This was one of those things which put Carol into Mommy space, and she liked that Ivy seemed to enjoy it just as much.

"Mommy, what is that?" Ivy asked as she saw the adult car seat when Carol opened the back door. Carol's SUV had the darkest legal tint, which meant that no one would be able to see Ivy in the back from outside of the car.

"It's for you, to make sure that you are safe when we go driving," Carol said, patting Ivy's bottom to indicate that she needed to get in the car. Ivy obeyed and climbed into the back, sitting down in her car seat and letting Carol pull the restraints over her chest and buckle her up.

"There, you aren't going to get away from

me, little miss," Carol said as she stroked Ivy's cheeks with her thumbs either side of her face and kissing her on her forehead before closing the door. Ivy felt her diaper push into her as the SUV roared into life and began driving toward Carol's house.

"Are you alright back there, honey," Carol said, looking in the rear-vision mirror and saw Ivy playing with her bunny.

"Yeah, Mommy," Ivy replied, enjoying how little, safe, and protected she felt. Carol smirked, seeing Ivy bounce her bunny over the side of the car as she tilted her head from side to side as she played. Carol felt her heart swell and wondered how lucky she was that Ivy was hers. She imagined forcing a vibrator into Ivy's diaper and locking her in place, making her take it as she drove around the city, her little girl a horny mess in the back, and the thought made her juices run.

Chapter 8

Ivy had fallen asleep in the back seat, and Carol smiled as she watched the young girl sucking on her paci and having her head tiled against one side of the car seat.

"Shh, it's just Mommy, baby girl," Carol said as Ivy woke up startled. Seeing Carol's loving face, Ivy resettled and let Carol carry her into her apartment. It was late, and Carol was happy there was no one about as she fumbled with the keys, Ivy's bag on her shoulder and her baby girl in her arms. Carol walked inside, locked the door, and sighed in contented bliss. This is what she had always wanted—a baby girl who was as enthralled by her as she was with her little one. Somebody who would let her experience and experiment all her deepest Mommy desires, and as Carol dropped Ivy's bag by the side of the bed, feeling her diaper become wet made her smile in satisfaction.

"What a good girl you are," Carol said to a sleeping Ivy, laying her down on the floor and beginning to change her wet diaper.

"Such a beautiful little girl," Carol added as she cleaned Ivy, powdered her, and put a fresh diaper on the girl's thin frame. Carol noticed that Ivy's ribs protruded less obviously, and she felt content that she was looking after her baby girl very well. Ivy opened her eyes to find Carol putting a new onesie on her and looked around the unfamiliar apartment, her eyes going wide.

"It's alright, little girl. You are in Mommy's house," Carol said, catching Ivy's eye and putting her at ease. Carol hadn't seen Ivy this little before, and she liked that Ivy was so comfortable that she could slip this deep into the space.

"I'm hungry now, Mommy," Ivy softly said, as she felt Carol rub over her diaper covered pussy affectionately.

"I thought you might be. Mommy is going

to make a bottle for you. Crawl behind me, little one. I want you to sit on Mommy's couch," Carol instructed, happy when Ivy sleepily obeyed. Carol made up a chocolate protein shake and walked over to where Ivy was sitting cross-legged on the couch.

"Come here," Carol instructed, cradling Ivy in her arms and pushing the nipple of the bottle between her lips.

"Such a good girl," Carol cooed as she watched Ivy hungrily drink. Carol liked that Ivy snuggling into her breast as she drank, making her nipples hard and wishing that she had milk of her own for Ivy.

"In the morning, I want to buy you a few new outfits and accessories, alright, baby?" Carol said, Ivy, nodding her head happily. She loved that Carol always wanted to make sure she had the best of everything. Ivy closed her eyes as she felt her tummy filling up and shook her head to dislodge the bottle from her lips.

"Don't fuss little one," Carol said, trying to

put the bottle back into her mouth, but Ivy continued to push it away.

"Are you finished, little girl?" Carol asked, trying not to become angry with Ivy. Ivy just nodded her head, and Carol smiled at the slight swelling of Ivy's tummy, patting it gently.

"I'm full, Mommy," Ivy said in the little voice, which always made Carol melt.

"Well, alright, then. But you need to tell Mommy when you have had enough. You almost got yourself a spanking because I thought you were being bratty," Carol explained, Ivy's eyes going wide.

"Yes, that's right. Mommy was almost about to turn you over and make that little bottom red," Carol said, turning Ivy over and playfully spanking her, making her giggle and squirm about on Carol's lap. Carol pinned Ivy to her thighs, making Ivy groan as the pressure of her full tummy was pushed down and made her have the hiccups.

"Oh, little one. Did Mommy play too

rough?" Carol teased, Ivy hiccupping again. Ivy nodded, and Carol pulled her onto her lap and patted her back as she rocked her gently.

Carol reluctantly left Ivy in the house Tuesday morning. After a night of holding onto her little girl, Carol felt that nothing could ruin her mood. She had left Ivy with a list of things to do so she didn't get bored and had set her phone up with the apartment's Wi-Fi. Getting messages all day from Ivy, Carol couldn't believe how wonderful her life had become. It was noticeable to the other girls' at work who benefitted from Carol's fantastic mood.

"I bought everyone donuts," Carol cheerily said as she walked into the staff lounge.

"Oh, yes," Gabi said, jumping up and down excitedly.

"You know. I don't care who she is. This girl is good for all of us!" Hope said with a mouthful of strawberry iced donuts.

"Yeah, she goes alright," Carol said,

remembering how sweet Ivy looked in the dino onesie Carol had dressed her in that morning.

"Actually. We haven't filled that receptionist position yet, have we?" Carol asked the girls who just shook their heads.

"Right. Well, I think I know just the girl," Carol said, winking at them and leaving the room.

"Do you think she's is going to give the job to her girlfriend?" Gabi asked Hope, who was busy getting another donut.

"I don't care, as long as she keeps bringing us treats, I don't care who she hires," Hope replied.

"Baby girl," Carol called as she walked into the apartment. She put her bag down and walked through the house until she found Ivy coloring in by the window. The breeze was making Ivy's hair catch the wind, making her look magnificent. Carol noticed that she had changed into the adult clothes Carol had permitted her to wear if she felt like going for a walk.

"Mommy!" Ivy exclaimed, looking up, squashing any doubt in Carol's mind as to which headspace Ivy was experiencing.

"Hey there, little one," Carol replied, coming to sit down next to Ivy and feeling her climb into her lap.

"Mommy's little angel," Carol said, wrapping Ivy in her arms and rocking her as she watched Ivy continue to color.

"I have a question for you, and you can say no, alright, baby girl," Carol said, making Ivy stop and turn her head to look at Carol, her big waiting eyes melting Carol's heart.

"How would you feel about coming to work with Mommy?" Carol asked, Ivy, tilting her head to the side and thinking.

"What do you mean?" Ivy said, putting her crayon down.

"Well. We need a receptionist. And I was wondering if you wanted to give that a go?

Mommy would be the one to train you as it is a small private practice, but I think you would really like it there. Plus, then you could write it on your resume, and it would give you some experience?" Carol suggested Ivy thought about it for a moment, shrugging her shoulders and feeling shy.

"Yeah, I guess. Would I fit in?" Ivy asked, making Carol's smile widen.

"Yeah, baby girl, you would fit in. We couldn't be too wrapped up in each other, even though the other girls know you are mine. They don't know that I am into this lifestyle, so any Mommy, baby dynamic would be off the table. But it would only be for when we are work. Once you get in the car, you'd be my little girl again," Carol explained, Ivy considering the offer.

"I didn't think I was ever going to be good enough to be a receptionist, Mommy," she said, making Carol laugh. She hadn't thought so highly of the job before. Not that she treated people differently based on their occupation, but she was amused at how highly Ivy clearly viewed it.

"Baby girl, you're going to be amazing! So, tomorrow you'll come with Mommy to work. I should maybe tell you. The girls call me Mama at work," Carol said, Ivy's head snapping back around to look at her dead in the eye.

"No, it's not like that. They don't mean it like the way you do. It's just that I am the oldest one there, and I am constantly helping them sort their shit out. So, when you hear them, you don't need to be jealous. You can call me Mama at work if you'd like, but you might need to pretend that you didn't know. Or you can call me Carol. It doesn't bother me either way. Alright?" Carol explained, half stumbling over her words, making Ivy laugh.

"Did you sort that out for yourself?" Ivy said, feeling less little and her usually adult sarcastic self once more. Carol noticed and raised an eyebrow, amused when Ivy wasn't put back in her place.

"Oh, so this is how you thank Mommy? You being a little smart ass?" Carol said, standing up and making Ivy fall off her lap, forcing her to stand up as well. Carol grabbed her wrist and walked quickly into her bedroom, shutting the door behind Ivy and pinning her against it. Carol had a cross, connected to the back of her door, and she cuffed Ivy's wrists above her head, and her ankles spread wide, locking her in place.

"I haven't had to punish you so far, I was wondering when this would happen," Carol said, making Ivy laugh.

"Oh, you won't be laughing in a moment, young lady," Carol said, kissing Ivy's forehead and slapping her panty covered pussy at the same time making her gasp.

"That's right," Carol said, rubbing Ivy's pussy, feeling her panties becoming wet with her juices.

"Such a ready little girl. Always horny for Mommy, aren't you?" Carol breathed into Ivy's ear, making her shiver and pull against the restraints.

"Where do you think you are going, little girl?" Carol teased as she slapped Ivy again, making her moan in pain and pleasure as Carol rubbed her sensually once more.

"Mommy," Ivy moaned, pushing her pussy out against Carol's hand only to be spanked again.

"Why are you moving like a little whore? Mommy doesn't want to fuck a whore tonight. Mommy wants her little princess," Carol said, pushing Ivy back and going to get a gag.

"I don't want to hear your complaints," she said, pushing the pacifier gag into Ivy's resisting mouth and strapping it in place.

"There. This might teach you to wear more than panties and a t-shirt around the house," Carol said, pinching Ivy's nipples and making her moan against the gag.

"Mommy can't hear you sugar," Carol said, taking Ivy's chin in her hand before shaking her head and letting her go. Taking a pair of nipple clamps from the drawer, Carol carefully put them on Ivy's hard nipples, over her t-shirt, concerned that she didn't want to push Ivy too much, but wanting to do exactly what she wanted with the girl. Carol could feel her pussy moisten, the slick juices making her full pussy lips wet. Taking her pants off, Carol also loosed her blouse, exposing her large breasts, cocooned in her emerald lace bra.

"Oh, I know you like the look of this," Carol said as she rubbed her breasts sensually in front of Ivy. Ivy watched, her eyes growing wide and becoming mesmerized by the woman in front of her. Carol felt her heart soften, making her smile and shake her head as she forgot for a minute that she was meant to be punishing Ivy.

"That's enough of that," Carol said, making her breasts bounce one final time before taking out her riding crop, instantly making Ivy strain against the cuffs.

"Baby girl, Mommy isn't going to hurt you

more than you can handle," Carol said, seeing the fear in Ivy's eyes. Although the idea of flogging was Ivy's, Carol was acutely aware that Ivy had been beaten by one of the foster parents she had had over the years. The look in Ivy's eyes told Carol that maybe even though she had said she was down for it, she might not be ready. Running the crop over Ivy's body, she saw Ivy fight back the tears, her fight to be freed, slowly ending, and Carol decided that she wasn't going to push Ivy on this tonight.

"Mommy's got you, baby girl," Carol said, throwing the crop on the floor and holding Ivy until her rigid body relaxed into Carol's loving arms. Ivy's breathing was shallow and frightened. Carol uncuffed Ivy's wrists, feeling her fling them around Carol's neck as she pulled herself closer to the woman who held her firmly.

"Mommy's here," Carol whispered.

"I'm sorry I was a smart ass," Ivy said as the tears rolled down her cheeks. Carol untied Ivy's ankles and went back to holding onto Ivy.

"And sorry I just cussed," Ivy added, realizing that she had broken another rule.

"Shh, little Ivy. Mommy can forgive that tonight," Carol said as she bought Ivy to the bathroom.

"Have a shower for Mommy," Carol said, turning the water on. She wanted Ivy to have some control over herself, and she sat down on the floor as she watched Ivy shower.

"I think I want to go and try the job, Mommy," Ivy said as she lathered her body with shower gel.

"I think that would be a good idea," Carol replied. Ivy got out of the shower and dried herself.

"I want to try it again," she softly said to Carol, who raised an eyebrow.

"Try what?" Carol said, patting the bed and waiting for Ivy to lay down on it. Carol began to diaper Ivy, giving her the bunny she loved so much to cuddle.

"I want to try the riding crop again. But

maybe not when I'm tied up," Ivy said, piquing Carol's concern.

"Why do you want to try?" Carol asked, pulling on a yellow fluffy diaper cover, Ivy's thigh-high white sockies, and putting a tight white t-shirt on her baby girl.

"You look like a cute little duckie," Carol said, cuddling Ivy.

"I want to try it because I think you like it, and I want you to be able to do things you like," Ivy replied, melting Carol's heart.

"That's so sweet, baby girl. But Mommy doesn't like it when you don't," Carol explained. Ivy frowned.

"But maybe I just didn't like it that way. Maybe I like it a different way?" Ivy replied, running out of the room and going to get the crop. Carol wondered if this was a good idea. The last thing she wanted to do was trigger Ivy, but her mind relaxed when Ivy came running back into the room.

"Here," Ivy said, handing Carol the riding

crop. Carol took it in her hands and immediately felt herself respond to it. She loved how it made her feel in control, if not somewhat cruel and sadistic.

"Maybe if I cuddle into you," Ivy suggested, Carol, opening her arms to the girl and enjoying the mix of primal desire and tender love she was experiencing.

"Suck your thumb, baby girl," Carol said in the low voice she always got when she was wildly aroused. Ivy obeyed, and Carol watched as Ivy's eyes grew wide like they always did when she was in little space. Carol replaced Ivy's thumb with her breast and moaned as the girl began to suckle eagerly.

"Good girl," Carol slowly said as she pulled her hair to one side and lightly patted Ivy's thigh with the crop. Ivy wriggled in her arms, only adding to Carol's enjoyment, and she brought the crop down harder into Ivy's soft skin, causing her to make high pitched squeals.

"This was a good idea, you clever little

girl," Carol said, kissing Ivy's forehead. Carol continued to gently mark Ivy's skin until it was red and hot, having to restrain herself from belting Ivy the way her pussy so desired.

In time, Carol said to herself as she watched Ivy painfully flinch.

"You are doing so good, baby girl. Come to Mommy's other side," Carol encouraged as she nursed Ivy in her other arm as her other hand began to claim Ivy's other thigh as her own.

"Mommy," Ivy said, wincing as she gasped and tried to pull away from Carol.

"It hurts," she added, making Carol moan in pleasure but stop herself from continuing.

"Oh, baby girl! You have been such a good girl for Mommy!" Carol said, putting the crop down and running lotion over Ivy's thighs. Ivy bashfully smiled.

"I wanted to be good for you. I liked it like that more than the first way," Ivy said, filling Carol with pride.

"I'm so proud of you for coming up with

this idea," she said as she patted Ivy's padded bottom.

"Come on. Come to the living room so Mommy can make us dinner, and you can play until then, alright, baby?" Carol said, picking Ivy up and carrying her out of the room.

Chapter 9

"What if they don't like me?!" Ivy nervously questioned on the way to work. Carol rolled her eyes. This was the seventh time they had had this decision that morning.

"Baby. What has Mommy said?" Carol answered, placing her hand under Ivy's skirt and rubbing her clit through her panties. Carol had made Ivy sit in the front passenger seat today to try and make her feel more grown-up.

"Mommy!" Ivy exclaimed, trying in vain to push Carol's hand away.

"This is Mommy's little pussy, and if I want to rub it, I'm going to damn well rub it. Now answer my question," Carol replied, enjoying how Ivy submitted and pushed her hips out to make it easier for Carol to play.

"That they will like me because they aren't bitches and that if anyone does something mean they have to answer to you," Ivy moaned as Carol slipped a finger into the entrance of Ivy's pussy.

"You are lucky we don't have time. Or I would pull over and make you take it before work, young lady," Carol said, causing Ivy's head to spin with desire. Pulling out of her quickly and kissing her cheek, Carol stopped the car.

"We are here, little one. From now on, call me Carol, is that understood Ivy?" Carol firmly said, Ivy, just nodding her head.

"Ok, here goes," Carol said, opening her door and waiting for Ivy to join her before locking the SUV and walking toward the building. Carol was nervous. She hadn't realized that just how young Ivy looked until she saw her reflection in the glass doors of the practice. She wondered if the girls would make fun of her or Ivy if they would give her a hard time or not, and she begged the universe that Hope wouldn't be cruel to her little girl.

"Hi, you must be Ivy?" Gabi said as they walked into the staff lounge.

"Yeah, hi," Ivy confidently replied.

"Pretty sweet that your girlfriend could hook you up with a job," Hope said as she turned around. Ivy just raised an eyebrow at her.

"She's good like that," Ivy replied, matching Hope's aggressive attitude and never breaking eye contact until Hope looked away.

Oh gosh, Carol thought to herself as she put her handbag away.

"So, this is where you can put your things. And we close the practice at 1 for lunch. It's an hour, and on Wednesdays, we go to the sushi place around the corner," Hope said, deciding that it was better to be friends than enemies.

"Ok cool," Ivy replied, smiling at her warmly.

I should have known she would be fine. She's been fighting all her life. She was always going to be fine, Carol said to herself, smiling to herself and shaking her head as she walked with Ivy to the front desk.

"You fucked Hope, didn't you, Carol?" Ivy

said as she sat down at the office chair, turning on the computer. Carol raised her eyebrows and bit her bottom lip, trying to hold back a smile but failing.

"I knew it! No one is that bitchy straight off the bat unless they are jealous!" Ivy quietly exclaimed, shocking Carol to hear her name from Ivy's lips.

"It was years ago, and it was only once. And I am going to have a really hard time letting you speak to me like I'm not your Mommy," Carol said, whispering the last part of her sentence, making Ivy beam.

"Don't push it," Carol warned, and she sat down next to Ivy and began teaching her the computer systems the practice used.

"Don't even think about it," Carol said as Ivy collapsed on the couch after the workday. Ivy's head hurt with all the information Carol had poured into it, and all she wanted to do was have a nap.

"I'm thinking about it," Ivy moaned into the couch cushions. It had only been a few days since Ivy's ex-boss exposed himself to her, and yet it felt like months ago. That's what Ivy had noticed the most when it came to Carol, time moved so slowly, and yet so fast at the same time.

"Well, maybe you should think about this instead," Carol said, walking into the living room, stroking her thick strap on dildo. She and Ivy had looked at it together online, but Ivy didn't know that Carol had actually bought it. Gasping, Ivy rolled onto her back and looked up at Carol.

"Open wide," Carol said, enjoying how Ivy obeyed so willingly.

"Make it wet, Mommy is going to fuck my frustration away, and you're little body is what I'm going to use to do it," Carol said, making Ivy giggle.

"Was it hard for you today, Mommy? To hear me laugh with the other girls and call you

Carol," Ivy teased, getting her nipple pinched until she yelped.

"Oh little girl, you asked for it," Carol replied, pulling Ivy's pants down quickly and parting her pussy lips, pressing the tip of the toy against her entrance.

"Little princess, it looks too big to fit," Carol playfully said, pinching Ivy's nipples again.

"Mommy can help with that," Carol teased, pouring lube over the toy and letting it drip down to Ivy's asshole, making her squirm.

"You can't get away from me, little one. Mommy is going to take you how I want to," Carol groaned as she pushed harder against Ivy, moaning in pleasure as Ivy's pussy was stretched open by the thick intruder.

"Such a tight little girl," Carol said, watching Ivy, making sure she didn't push her too far. Carol began to fuck her, rocking her hips back and forth, keeping the rhythm constant as Ivy became accustomed to the sensation.

"You like it, don't you, little girl?" Carol

questioned, feeling Ivy's muscle relax and take her more easily.

"Yes, Mommy. Oh, Mommy, I love it," Ivy replied, bucking her hips and giving Carol all the encouragement she needed. She pinned Ivy's hips down and drilled her, turning her sweet girl into a moaning mess as she pounded the young girl's pussy.

"You aren't allowed to cum, little girl," Carol said, making Ivy's eyes pop open and moan in agony.

"But Mommy," Ivy complained, feeling dangerously close to orgasm. Carol put a pacifier in Ivy's mouth and placed her hand on her throat.

"Mommy said no," Carol replied, feeling Ivy try to hold back an orgasm but failing like Carol had hoped she would. Continuing to fuck her, Carol could feel Ivy's juices drip around the dildo with every thrust.

"Such a dirty little girl," Carol moaned as her own orgasm flooded her being making her shiver and her nipples got hard as the frustration of the day was fucked away. She continued to use Ivy as her second, third, and the fourth orgasm took over her, finally pulling out as she panted heavily. She placed her hand over Ivy's used pussy and felt Ivy curl into her arms.

"You are leaking, beautiful," Carol said, feeling Ivy's juices coating her hand. Carol got up and took off the strap on, stripped herself and Ivy naked, and took them both to the shower.

Chapter 10

Ivy spent the rest of the week learning all about the programming systems, interacting with clients, and navigating the staff lounge. She and Hope had made peace, and Hope had even invited Ivy out for drinks with her and Gabi after work on Friday.

"I don't know if I should go, Mommy," Ivy said Thursday night. Carol had made Ivy a bubble bath and was busy washing her hair. She had made it especially lovely tonight by dimming the lights. Ivy's eyes became sensitive at night, and she loved that Carol remembered.

"What are you scared about, baby?" Carol replied, rinsing Ivy's hair. Ivy picked up some bubbles and blew them into the air.

"What if they are mean and just wanted to get me away from you so that you can't tell them to stop?" Ivy explained, making Carol's heart melt.

"You are such a sweet little girl underneath all that makeup and eyeliner," Carol said, wiping Ivy's face clean.

"But what if, Mommy?" Ivy said instantly. Carol held Ivy's face in both her hands and looked her dead in the eye.

"Has Mommy ever let you down?" Carol asked. Ivy pretended to think, making Carol scoff.

"No, Mommy," Ivy giggly replied.

"Right, so if you feel that it isn't going the way, you want it to or thought it would. What are you going to do?" Carol asked.

"Call Mommy," Ivy replied before standing up in the tub.

"Good girl," Carol replied, taking a towel down from the rack and drying Ivy's body.

"Mommy, guess what?" Ivy replied as Carol began to diaper her.

"What, darling?" Carol said, holding up two onesie options and letting Ivy choose.

"It's my birthday next week," Ivy said, pointing at the blue on with the puppy on the front. Carol smiled and looked at Ivy with nothing but love in her eyes.

"Well, Mommy will have to give you a special day then, won't I?" Carol replied, watching as Ivy stood and followed her into the living room.

"I've never had something special for my birthday before," Ivy said as Carol took the nuggets out of the oven and into Ivy's bowl. She added a little container of sauce to the bowl and placed it into Ivy's lap. Carol went back to the kitchen and took her plate of seafood paella and came to sit next to Ivy.

"What do you want to do for your birthday, then, little girl? I think we should do something little, and something grown-up," Carol suggested making Ivy clap her hands.

"Yes, please, Mommy," Ivy replied, snuggling into Carol.

"Eat your nuggies, baby girl. We can look

online tonight to see where you want to go," Carol said, feeding Ivy a nugget and watching as she cuddled up to her while they watched the news.

"I think he is really hot!" Gabi exclaimed Friday night at the loud Bowling Alley. Ivy felt embarrassed that they couldn't go out clubbing because she was underage but thought it was really lovely that the girls' didn't seem to care. Carol had dropped Ivy off and given her strict instructions that she was to call her if things went downhill. Ivy loved that about Carol; she was always so supportive and loving.

"Well, his bowling sucks," Ivy said, replying to Gabi, making Hope laugh.

"I don't think it's his bowling that she is impressed with," Hope said before dramatically eating a chip. The guy that they were loudly talking about heard them and walked over, winking at Gabi before taking a bowling ball from their section.

"Oh, that's all I needed," Gabi playfully said before going over to talk to him, leaving Hope and Ivy alone.

"Well, we can't even play without her, and it's her turn!" Ivy exclaimed, taking a sip of her soda.

"Yeah, whatever, we will just wait for her. So tell me, did you grow up around here?" Hope asked. Ivy had been hoping that she wouldn't have to keep retelling her story; it made her cringe.

"No, I'm from out of town. I moved here this year," Ivy replied, watching Gabi flirt with the boy.

"And, you and Carol met how?" Hope asked, making Ivy's head turn back to her.

"At a café," Ivy replied, not wanting to give away too much information.

"You know. Carol and I fucked once. But I guess she likes younger girls, so it didn't work out," Hope said. Ivy just nodded her head.

"Yeah, I don't really care what you guys

did," Ivy said, watching the lights at the bowling alley flicker and shine.

"Are you worried that as you get older, Carol will leave you for a younger girl?" Hope pressed. Ivy felt herself getting angry. Of course, she had thought of that. She didn't need Hope to bring it up as well.

"Hope, get fucked," Ivy said, standing up and heading towards the entrance. Hope stayed sitting in the booth, somewhat impressed with herself that she had made Ivy crack so easily.

Ivy walked out onto the street. She wasn't sure where she was going, but she just needed to keep walking. She took out her phone, deciding that she would ring Carol when she got to wherever she was going. Passing the bars, she wished she could go in, passing the type of restaurants that Carol loved and across the street to a pizza joint. She kept walking, passed a cupcake store which sold marvelous creations, and found herself in a trendy looking diner downtown.

"Hi, what can I get you?" The curvy Latina

woman behind the counter asked. Ivy just shrugged her shoulders looked around for a menu.

"Here, sweetie," the woman said, handing her a menu and pouring her an espresso.

"Thanks, Ma'am," Ivy sadly replied, making the woman laugh.

"Oh, honey, call me Nancy," Nancy replied, making Ivy smile faintly.

"Ok, Nancy," she replied. Satisfied, Nancy walked to the other end of the counter and began talking to other customers. Ivy liked the woman's warm smile and loving eyes and made her Miss Carol. Taking out her phone, she saw that Carol was ringing her.

"Hey," Ivy said down the phone. She looked around, half expecting Carol to be somewhere looking at her.

"Baby, what happened? Hope messaged me saying that you stormed out?" Carol questioned. Ivy liked that there was concern and not anger in her voice.

"You were meant to ring Mommy if something was wrong," she added. Ivy bit her bottom lip and tilted her head as Nancy place a slice of pie down in front of her.

"I didn't order this?" Ivy questioned, unsure as to why Nancy had done that.

"I know, but trust me, you're going to like it," Nancy replied, winking at Ivy before disappearing once again.

"I know I was meant to ring. I was just so angry I didn't want to ring you when I was that mad. I just needed to walk. I'm in some diner downtown. It's actually really nice. If I send you my location, could you come and get me, please?" Ivy asked. Carol understood why Ivy hadn't called and nodded her head as she listened to the story.

"Of course, baby girl. It's getting late. I don't want you move from that spot, alright?" Carol instructed Ivy, taking a bite of the pie and raising her eyebrows.

"Ok," Ivy replied, making Carol laugh.

"What are you missing, my love?" Carol asked. Ivy gave a sideward smile before biting her bottom lip.

"Ok, Mommy," Ivy whispered, making Carol smirk.

"There's my good girl. Sit tight. Mommy is on her way," Carol replied, hanging up the phone.

"So, what do you think?" Nancy said as she poured Ivy a hot chocolate. Ivy smiled at her. She had that same loving eyes that Carol did, and it made her wonder if she had them because she was a Mommy as well or if it was just because that was her face.

"Pretty good," Ivy replied, making Nancy laugh.

"Pretty good?!" She exclaimed faining pretend disbelief. Ivy giggled and took a sip of the hot chocolate.

"This, however, is really good," Ivy said, taking another sip.

"Well, it's the secret ingredient that makes

it soo good," Nancy said as she saw Ivy's big puppy dog eyes and smiled.

"What is it?" Ivy asked, feeling her anger go away, and her guard go down. Nancy put two marshmallows into the mug before raising an eyebrow at Ivy.

"Well, if I told you, it wouldn't be a secret anymore," Nancy said, winking at her and smiling at Carol, who came to sit next to Ivy. Gasping, Ivy wrapped her arms around Carol and held her tight.

"I see you've been busy," Carol laughed as she saw the selection of treats in front of Ivy.

"I had time," Ivy replied, letting Carol go and sitting up.

"So, tell me what happened," Carol said, taking a bite of the pie and moaning in appreciation.

"Have you tried this?!" Carol asked, taking another bite.

"See that, that is the correct response," Nancy laughed as she walked passed.

"Yeah, I have, it's good," Ivy replied, Carol, pausing and looking at her as though she had lost her mind.

"Good?! It's a lot better than good," Carol said, deciding that she was going to finish the pie herself.

"So?" Carol pressed, wanting to know how Ivy had ended up downtown.

"So, everything was going fine. In fact, it was really fun. But then Gabi went off to flirt with some guy, and Hope started asking me all these questions. I answered most of them, but then she bought up that you guys and messed around and that you only like young girls and that when I get too old, you'll probs dump me for a younger girl. So I told her to fuck off," Ivy said before picking up her hot chocolate and holding it in both hands as she drank.

"Right. I'm not going to dump you because you get older. For goodness sake, that is the creepiest thing I have ever heard. It makes me sound like a pervert!" Carol exclaimed, shaking her head.

"Yeah, but like, it just made me so mad. Coz I had thought that maybe that would happen and when she said it I just like, got really angry," Ivy tried to explain. Carol placed her hand on her chest, and looked at Ivy, slightly hurt that she would have those thoughts.

"Oh, baby girl," Carol said, wrapping her arms around Ivy.

"Mommy is never going to leave you," she whispered in Ivy's ear, causing Ivy to snuggle into the crook of Carol's neck, a few tears escaping.

"Alright?" Carol questioned, watching as Ivy nodded her head and fought the urge to suck her thumb.

"Maybe we need to get you into a sport or something to find some better friends. I don't think I want those girls' hanging around you when I am not there," Carol said, standing up and kissing Ivy on the top of her head before going to pay.

Chapter 11

Carol took Ivy home, Ivy falling asleep in the car within minutes.

"Come on, baby girl," Carol said as she gently woke Ivy up and held her hand as they walked inside.

"Mommy, can we plan my birthday now?" Ivy asked, Carol, smiling down at her.

"Not tonight, I want you ready for bed, and then you are going to nurse until you fall asleep," Carol said, helping Ivy take off her clothes and running a shower for her.

"Ok, Mommy," Ivy said, getting up the warm water and quickly showering.

Carol dressed Ivy in a black diaper cover and a loose white shirt, setting her up in the living room on a blanket on the floor as Carol changed into her pajamas.

"I thought you might like this," Carol said, only coming back into the room wearing long pajama pants and rubbing her full breasts. Sitting on the couch, Carol patted the spot next to her and smiled as Ivy crawled over to her.

"Up you come," Carol said as she lifted Ivy onto her lap and sighed in content bliss as she felt Ivy begin to nurse.

"Such a good girl for Mommy," Carol said, patting Ivy's padded bottom as she rocked her.

"You are perfect, little Ivy. You will always be Mommy's beautiful little girl. No matter how old you are," Carol whispered as Ivy looked up at her with her big eyes and long lashes.

"Shh, close your eyes, honey. Time to sleep," Carol said, placing her hand over Ivy's eyes and stroking her forehead, feeling Ivy suckle slower until only her lips were pursed against Carol's nipple.

"Mommy? Can we do it now?!" Ivy asked as sitting at the end of the bed, waiting for Carol to wake up.

"I fear how many more times I will have to tell you no if we don't just do it now!" Carol laughed, opening her arms and having Ivy snuggle into them.

"So I've had a few thoughts," Ivy said, taking out of her phone and showing Carol her image boards.

"You have been busy! When have you had time for all this?" Carol laughed. Ivy just rolled her eyes.

"It doesn't take that much time, Mommy," Ivy said, scrolling through the images.

"You want to hike up a mountain and have a picnic at the top? That's cute. I can get you a cute little hiking outfit!" Carol said, imagining how irresistible Ivy would look. Ivy just rolled her eyes.

"I think you might be too tired once we get to the top, Mommy," Ivy said, worried that Carol wouldn't be able to keep up.

"Don't let this fool you, Mommy is both

stronger and fitter than you," Carol said, winking at Ivy and making her blush. Carol just smirked.

"We need to go present shopping. You're going to have a budget. I think $200 for little things and $400 for big girl things because big girl things are more expensive," Carol said, explaining herself when she saw Ivy open her mouth to speak, assuming that it was to protest the amounts.

"I wasn't about to complain! I was about to say that it doesn't need to be that much!" Ivy said, enjoying how Carol just shrugged her shoulders.

"Well, it is, so there enjoy," Carol laughed, causing Ivy to cover her in kisses.

"If I had known I'd get this reaction, I'd buy your affection more often," Carol laughed as she felt Ivy's hand slip into her pants.

"I'm not your whore. You can't pay me to fuck you," Ivy sensually whispered, making Carol chuckle.

"That's some very grown-up language for

someone wearing a diaper," Carol said, pulling Ivy onto her thigh.

"Then," Ivy said, quickly taking it off, along with her shirt.

"Better?" Ivy teased feel Carol take back control and roll her onto her back.

"Now it is," Carol said, placing her hand on Ivy's pussy and making quick work of turning her into a moaning mess.

"That was not my plan," Ivy moaned as she felt Carol begin to kiss her neck.

"It happens," Carol laughed as she pushed her fingers into Ivy and took her over the edge.

"Oh, you make it too easy for Mommy," Carol said as she replaced her hand with her thigh and pressed Ivy's clit into it, refusing to let her come down from one orgasm as another one built within her.

"You're so mean," Ivy said, trying in vain to overpower Carol.

"I told you Mommy was stronger than you little girl," Carol whispered as she wrapped Ivy in her arms and continued to hump her.

"Mommy," Ivy said, pushing Carol away as she came over Carol's thigh, gripping into the older woman's skin and leaving red marks on her as she felt herself moisten her thigh.

"Well, I know how you can thank Mommy," Carol said, ripping the bed sheets off her and Ivy and kicking off her pajama pants. Carol toyed with her cunt, pulling her lips wide and pushing Ivy's head down.

"Get busy, little one," Carol said, holding Ivy's head to her cunt and rubbing it over her face, moaning as she felt Ivy's tongue taste her pussy juices. Ivy loved how Carol tasted and lapped at her cunt, causing Carol to moan and play with her breasts as she flooded Ivy's mouth.

"You were horny today, Mommy," Ivy giggled as she wiped her mouth on the bedsheets before coming up and cuddling with Carol.

"Yeah, I was actually," Carol chuckled to herself, surprised at how quickly she came.

That afternoon, Carol and Ivy went to the mall in search of Ivy's gifts. Ivy liked that they went together, and when the stores were only a few hours till closing. She didn't want to go during the peak shopping times because large numbers of people made her feel uneasy. Ivy loved that Carol never made a fuss about the few things Ivy really needed from her, and as they walked through the mall, a large fluffy pink blanket caught Ivy's eye.

"Oh, this is so nice!" Ivy said, running her fingers over it. Carol smiled and looked around the store. She had to admit. Ivy did have good taste in linen and soft furnishings.

"I think I need this," Ivy said, the store assistant coming over to help her.

"It's your birthday. You can get anything you want, honey," Carol said. Ivy also bought a pair of fluffy pajama shorts, and she smirked at Carol when she said she needed to get a bigger size.

"For my diaper," Ivy whispered, Carol,

smirking and enjoying what a sweet girl she had to call her own. They went from store to store, looking at everything from activewear to technology, custom-designed stuffies, and animated backpacks. After hours of searching and buying, Ivy was finally ready to go home.

"This was so much fun, Mommy!" Ivy exclaimed as Carol put her into her car seat. They had carked around the block from the mall so that Carol could put Ivy in it today.

"I'm glad you had such a good day, baby girl. You can't have your presents until your birthday though. And if you complain, I'll return all of them," Carol said, seeing what Ivy was about to ask.

"Ok, Mommy," Ivy said, reaching for her paci and blankie.

"There's my good girl," Carol cooed before she closed the door and walked around to the driver's seat.

Ivy could hardly wait the two days until her

birthday. She was so excited at how her life had turned out and so delighted that Carol was her girlfriend and Mommy and as she lay in bed next to Carol on the last night as an 18-year-old, she thought of all the times where she wanted more than anything to give up and just accept defeat. As she looked over and snuggled into Carol, she was so happy that she kept going and kept believing that she could create a beautiful life for herself.

"Happy Birthday, baby girl," Carol whispered in her ear. Ivy blinked her eyes open and looked around.

"Mommy," Ivy happily said. Carol kissed her forehead and felt her diaper.

"Let's get you changed, little one. What type of day do you want today? Your big girl one or your baby girl one?" Carol asked. They had decided to celebrate Ivy's birthday over two days. Each day dedicated to one of her main headspaces.

"Baby girl, one!" Ivy said as she flung her

arms in the air.

"I had a feeling you would pick that one," Carol laughed as she placed Ivy on the floor and changed her.

Dressing her in a fresh diaper, a pair of black denim overalls with a light pink t-shirt underneath, and black ankle socks, Carol sat her up at the kitchen bench.

"Alright, let's have a yummy fruit platter for breakfast, and then you can open your presents," Carol said as Ivy clapped her hands. Carol had cut up melon in the shape of stars, strawberries dipped in chocolate, and there was also a range of other berries. Ivy's eyes went wide.

"Mommy, this is delicious!" Ivy said, finishing her breakfast quickly.

"Easy there, tiger. You're going to get a sore tummy if you eat that fast," Carol said, pulling Ivy's plate away from her and giving her a warning look.

"Sorry, Mommy, I just want to open my

presents!" Ivy exclaimed.

"You won't be able to open them because you'll feel sick and need a nap if you keep that up," Carol said, giving Ivy her plate back and watching as she tried to eat slowly.

"Oh, this is just too painful. Down you get," Carol laughed, letting Ivy walk over to the collection of presents on the coffee table. Carol had set up balloons and streamers over the table, and Ivy played with the balloons until Carol came over and pulled her into her lap and took the first present down.

"Do you want Mommy to help you, or can you do it by yourself, little one?" Carol asked, placing the colorfully wrapped box in Ivy's lap.

"I can do it, Mommy," Ivy replied, resting her head back on Carol's shoulder as she ripped the packaging off. Although Ivy knew what she was getting, it didn't stop her from being excited and giggling as she saw the wooden train set she unwrapped.

"We can set it up in the living room if you

like, honey," Carol said, Ivy, nodding her head as she reached for another gift. Slowly, Ivy unwrapped everything, the colorful paper surrounding them as she opened the last gift, her pink fluffy blanket.

"Mommy, this is the best birthday I have ever had," Ivy said, cuddling into Carol with her blankie in her arms.

"I'm glad you have liked it so far, baby girl," Carol said as she kissed Ivy all over her face.

"But it's not over yet, little one," Carol said, causing Ivy to look at her in confusion.

"What do you mean?" Ivy asked, reaching for her custom-designed bear and sparkly pink ball.

"Well, I thought it might be nice for you to have a little play with all your new toys, and then we will have a nap, and after we can out for ice-cream and come back for your cake. And you can decide what we have for dinner as well," Carol said, watching as Ivy tried to comprehend her words.

"Mommy," Ivy said, bursting into tears. Carol had wondered when this would happen. Ivy had cried when she was overwhelmed with happiness on more than one occasion.

"It's alright, little one. Mommy's got you. This is what good girls get for their birthday, and you are the best girl in the world," Carol loving said, letting Ivy cry in her arms until she began to calm down.

"Are you alright little one?" Carol asked as Ivy nodded her head and wiped her tears away.

"And we haven't even got to tomorrow yet!" Carol said, making Ivy laugh.

"Maybe we can wait for a day or two, Mommy?" Ivy said, Carol, kissing the top of her head and agreeing with the look in her eyes.

"So, you have a little play now, baby girl. Mommy is going to tidy all this up, and then we can have lunchies, a nap, and then go out in the afternoon," Carol said as Ivy began to build up her train set.

Chapter 12

Ivy woke up early the next morning and tiptoed out into the kitchen and sat up at the table, ready to make her creation. She used all the glitters that she had and giggled as she watched her picture come to life, even getting glitter on her face.

"I made it for you, Mommy," Ivy proudly said as she held up the glittery picture for Carol to see. Carol smiled at her as she walked down the corridor and wrapped her dressing gown around her waist.

"Let me see," Carol sleepily said as she sat on the couch and let Ivy snuggle in next to her.

"It's Mommy and Ivy at the store picking out presents," Ivy said, pointing to the glittery figures. Carol kissed the top of Ivy's head and looked at the picture.

"I love this," Carol softly said, a tear

rolling down her cheek, confusing Ivy.

"Then why are you crying, Mommy?" She asked, taking the picture out of Carol's hands and frowning curiously at her.

"This is the first picture I've ever been given. I guess I wasn't expecting it get to me so much," Carol replied, wiping her eyes.

"So, does that mean you like it?" Ivy playfully said as she looked up at Carol, making her laugh.

"Yes, it does. And I have just decided that you need a lot more craft supplies to make even more," Carol said, taking the picture and putting it on the fridge.

"But not today," Ivy replied, hoping that her day of big girl things wasn't off the table.

"No," Carol said, spinning on the spot, a wicked gleam in her eye.

"Definitely not today," Carol said, eyeing Ivy up and down.

"I see that you are already dressed," Carol said. Although Ivy had gotten into little space easily to make Carol the picture, she had dressed in her adult clothes while Carol was sleeping. Her black jeans, white sneakers, and grey hoodie still made her look like a little girl with her messy ponytail and black denim jacket.

"Nothing gets passed you. So, Carol, what have you got planned for today?" Ivy said, enjoying the few times she was permitted to call Carol by her first name. Carol raised an eyebrow, finding it harder to adjust but loving her flirtatious naughty girl all the same.

"Get your ass off the bench," Carol said, slapping Ivy's thighs and making her sit on a bench stool instead.

"See, I'm still Mommy," Carol teased, taking Ivy's chin in her hand and shaking her head, making her giggle.

"Maybe," Ivy replied, taking out her phone and posting a selfie.

"You need to hurry up and eat something because we have a few things to pick up before lunch," Carol said, wanting to get out of the house as soon as possible.

"I thought you were going to make my breakfast?" Ivy asked, making Carol laugh.

"Oh no, big girl, Mommy is gone until tonight. Get yourself something before you starve," Carol playfully replied, winking at Ivy before taking her coffee and disappearing out of sight. Ivy rolled her eyes and went to the cupboard, taking out a bowl, spoon, cereal, and milk. Munching on her breakfast loudly, Ivy followed Carol as she fluttered around the kitchen, living room, and bedroom.

"You're going to get a tummy ache if you don't sit down," Carol said, putting in her earrings as Ivy put her sunglasses on her head with one hand, her spoon in her mouth and her cereal almost spilling.

"Yes, Mommy," Ivy said, ignoring her suggestion but enjoying how it felt to be able to do whatever she wanted and to have Carol's loving care still.

"Fine, get sick, see if I care," Carol said,

putting her scarf on and slapping Ivy's ass.

"You care," Ivy whispered as she sat in Carol's lap and finished her breakfast. Loving how it felt to have Carol wrap her loving arms around her as she ate, Ivy melted into the embrace and felt herself becoming content in a blissful state she was slowly getting used to.

"Mommy?" Ivy asked, wanting Carol's attention.

"Yes, baby girl," Carol replied, stroking Ivy's arms.

"Can I wear a diaper on my big girl day?" Ivy asked, making Carol smile.

"Of course, little one," Carol replied, secretly loving that Ivy still wanted little things when she was about to go out and buy a diamond necklace.

"You're just, Mommy's little girl, aren't you?" Carol asked as she took the bowl away from Ivy and turned her into her, holding her lovingly, and Ivy looked up and into her eyes and nodded.

Carol had dressed Ivy in a pair of denim jeans and a tight white t-shirt that showed her tummy, a pink bow in her hair, and a pair of street sneakers.

"You look cute," Carol said as Ivy twirled for her before sitting on the bed and watching Carol get dressed.

"Mommy, not that one," Ivy said as Carol took out a pullover.

"What's wrong with this one?" Carol said, looking at the cream-colored pullover. Ivy just gigged and got up, taking down her favorite pullover that Carol owned.

"Oh, I see," Carol said as Ivy held it up to her. Ivy smirked and sat back down, looking at Carol suggestively.

"Don't look at me like that unless you want trouble, young lady. I am not about to have us be late for your first surprise of the day," Carol warned as Ivy lay back on the bed and spread her thighs. Carol walked over to Ivy and slowly dressed herself before patting between Ivy's thighs.

"Anyway, baby girls don't get fucked," Carol said, making Ivy pout.

"But, Mommy, I am so horny, please?" Ivy begged amusing Carol, who shook her head no.

"And don't even think about it," Carol said as Ivy tried to put her hand down her pants. Carol grabbed Ivy's wrist and pulled her to her feet.

"Is Mommy going to have to punish you, little girl?" Carol asked as Ivy squirmed to get away from her.

"No," Ivy pouted, standing still and snuggling into Carol before sucking her thumb.

"Maybe if you're a good girl for me, I'll let you show me how badly you want it," Carol said, patting Ivy on the bottom before leading her towards the car.

Carol had a day full of cafes and shopping planned, and as she unbuckled Ivy from her car seat, she could tell that Ivy was fidgety.

"What is it, baby?" Carol asked as they held hands and walked into a jewelry store.

"What if people can tell I am wearing a diaper?" Ivy whispered as she looked at the rings in the cabinet.

"They can't, don't worry, baby. I wouldn't do that to you," Carol said as she double-checked. It was true, the diaper she had put Ivy in today was thin, and her loose jeans made it impossible to tell what she had on underneath. They looked through the store, Ivy finally deciding on a ring she liked before they continued through the mall. Ivy didn't know what it was, but something was hurting her heart. It wasn't a feeling she had felt for a long time, and as she walked with Carol through the stores, she felt herself becoming more and more dissociated. She smiled and talked to Carol like nothing was wrong, but knew that something was going on, even if she couldn't put her finger on it.

Eventually, Carol was buckling Ivy back up in her car seat and kissed her on the cheek before going into the driver's side and driving back home. Ivy wondered if Carol could tell that she was faking it, almost like she was watching someone else's life, and not being able to feel any of the feelings she thought she should.

You've just gone on a huge shopping spree. You should be happy. No one has ever treated you this good, what's the matter with you? Ivy thought to herself. She looked out the window and wished that she could disappear. She felt sick like a knot was forming in her tummy that she couldn't seem to unravel.

"Baby?" Carol said, breaking Ivy's train of thought. Ivy looked up to notice that they were in the driveway, Carol looking at Ivy inquisitively, clearly having asked her a question.

"Huh?" Ivy replied, Carol, getting out of the car and walking around to open her door.

"Baby girl, what's wrong?" Carol said, unbuckling Ivy's seat belt.

"I don't know," Ivy whispered in response, making Carol smile understandably.

"It's alright, baby. I know that maybe today was a bit much," Carol said as she picked up the handful of bags and took Ivy's hand in her other hand. Ivy just nodded her head and began to cry.

"Shh. It's alright, baby girl, Mommy's here," Carol said as she took Ivy inside. She dropped the bags by the door and took Ivy to the couch, sitting down and letting her snuggle up next to her.

"Mommy's sweet girl," Carol said as Ivy grabbed at her softly.

I bet she is overwhelmed because last time she had a birthday, she was running away from home. She's probably never had somebody treat her so well, and I guess it was all a bit too much for her, Carol thought to herself as she felt Ivy's breathing be shallow and fast.

"Do you know what you need to feel better, baby girl?" Carol asked, watching as Ivy shook her head no.

"How about a hot bath and a nap?" Carol suggested. Ivy just shrugged her shoulders. She wasn't sure what she needed or wanted. All she knew was that she didn't want to feel like this anymore.

"Mommy," Ivy softly said, reaching for Carol, who scooped her up and carried her to the bathroom.

"Down you go," Carol said, lowering Ivy to the floor and beginning to undress her.

"Such a beautiful little girl," Carol said, putting a paci in Ivy's mouth. Carol began to undress Ivy. She dimmed the lights and put on a soft melodied soundtrack before continuing to take Ivy's clothes off.

"I'm sorry, Mommy. I don't know why I feel like this," Ivy softly said as tears rolled down her cheeks.

"Oh, sweetie, it's ok. Sometimes the world just gets a bit too much," Carol said, understanding that Ivy wasn't being bratty or ungrateful. She was simply triggered by the feeling of being loved at this level because it was so different from what her whole life had been like. Even though they had been together for a year, Carol knew that Ivy would probably have many more moments like this as their relationship progressed and deepened.

"Ok, let's get you into this water," Carol whispered, taking Ivy's hand and leading her into tub and watching as she brought her knees up to her chest.

"Do you want to lay on your tummy, that way the water is all over you?" Carol suggested, Ivy, moving her body under Carol's direction.

"Thanks for looking after me, Mommy," Ivy whispered, smiling for the first time in hours and feeling her body come back into balance.

"That's what I'm here for baby girl. To make sure that you are looked after and that nothing bad happens to you," Carol replied, sitting down next to the tub as Ivy brought her face to rest on Carol's thighs, wetting her jeans.

"It's ok, baby," Carol lovingly said as Ivy looked up, worry in her eyes that Carol would be angry with her.

Carol gently poured warm water down Ivy's back, giving her shivers and making her giggle.

"There's my happy girl," Carol loving remarked as she saw the sparkle start to come back to Ivy's eyes. Ivy reached her arms up, Carol having to think twice before taking her shirt off.

"Do you need Mommy cuddles, little one?" Carol said, undressing, and stepping into the tub. Ivy nodded as she watched Carol sit down and started to snuggle into her once she was under the water.

"I don't ever want you to leave me, Mommy," Ivy said as she nestled her head into Carol's neck.

"Oh, baby girl. Mommy is never leaving you," Carol replied and kissing down Ivy's collar bone and making her giggle.

"Don't Mommy," Ivy whined, encouraging Carol.

"Or what baby girl," Carol teased, hoping that Ivy was in the mood for more than cuddles.

"Or I'm gonna get all tingling," Ivy replied, blushing and trying to push Carol away.

"Maybe that's what I want," Carol said, grabbing Ivy's wrists and pulling her back toward her and wrapping her arms around her.

"I'm glad that you feel better, baby," Carol said as Ivy straddled her thighs and felt the water on her clit as her thighs were spread, opening her pussy and causing her hips to react.

"Can somebody feel the warmth of the water on their pussy baby," Carol said, intuitively knowing what was happening. Ivy bit her bottom lip and nodded her head. Carol smirked and decided that she wanted Ivy horny and unsatisfied tonight. She had only just got Ivy back to feel happy. She didn't want her to become overwhelmed again.

"Let's get you, dry baby girl," Carol said, getting out of the water before drying herself and then Ivy.

"I want you," Ivy said, making Carol laugh, feeling Ivy's hands begin to touch her body.

"I can see that. But you know what baby girl, not tonight. Tonight I want you all wrapped up in a blankie and snuggling next to Mommy. Alright, little one?" Carol said, taking Ivy's wrist in her hand and leading her to the bedroom. Ivy, who was clearly disappointed by Carol's plans, just nodded her head, not wanting to be bratty for her Mommy.

"There's my good girl," Carol said, beginning to diaper Ivy and put her in a light blue onesie. Carol watched as Ivy got comfy in bed as she pulled on her pajamas and got into bed with Ivy.

"Mommy's snuggly little girl," Carol cooed, pulling the blankets around the both of them and tucking Ivy into bed.

"Mommy?" Ivy softly whined, tugging on Carol's t-shirt. Carol smiled down at Ivy.

"Do you want to use your big girl words,

baby?" Carol asked, beginning to pull her shirt up. Ivy just shook her head, making Carol smile at her lovingly before settling her as she nursed.

"Beautiful girl," Carol said, watching Ivy be little in her arms, enjoying the feeling of being the person Ivy needed the most.

Who is Tina Moore?

Tina Moore has enjoyed the lifestyle of a Mommy Domme for several years. She began secretly exploring kink and BDSM in her youth and found her love of being a strict Mommy Domme in early 2000.

Tina Moore slowly became more comfortable and confident through making friends in the community and exploring the lifestyle and now openly celebrates being a Mommy Domme to her little.

Before becoming an author, Tina Moore worked in the finance sector, but it was through the encouragement of her current little that she took the leap and wrote her first MDLG book, Nancy's Little One.

From then on, Tina Moore continued to combine her experiences and desires, as well as the sweet and naughty things her baby girl does, to bring you tantalizing and salacious stories about both MDLG and DDLG relationships and the ABDL littles and middles who enjoy them.

Follow her on:

Author Page on Amazon

Instagram @tinamoore.kdp